Bill Driedger's *Out of the* introduces understanding of description of events invite th is a winner!

y and skillful ; book

MW00963323

Reuben Epp
Author and Scholar of Low German

Bill Driedger writes of a way of life now gone, and he does so with brilliant insight, humour and compassion ... Driedger's stories provide an understanding of a group of pioneers whose heirs have built on their foundation to make Western Canadian society what it is.

Dave Hubert
Amateur historian, educator and author

Through the eyes of Jakob, the early life, joys and struggles of the Old Colony come alive. Bill Driedger's memory is sharp and concise but it is his ability to get to the heart of the day-to-day experiences which invite the reader into a different time and place. While life was simpler then, as Driedger depicts, it was no less complex. Told with a purity of line and simplicity of style, this evocative work stirs our humanity to a new level of understanding.

Rev. B. Joan Lawrence
Retired priest and hospital chaplain

Authentic, descriptive and insightful, *Jakob, Out of the Village* is ... a "must read" novel for all those younger Mennonite generations who desire to get in touch with their roots ... Bill Driedger has drawn from his personal experiences to capture the cultural nuances as well as the struggles faced by the children of immigrant parents in rural Saskatchewan.

Tony Nickel, PhD
Professor Emeritus, University of Regina

The author's sparse writing style—clear, compact and unadorned—is very much like the Old Colony Mennonites themselves ... the humorous incidents in the book demonstrate the peasant wisdom of the Old Colony people

Archivist, Mennonite Historical Sc

Jakob

out of the village

william driedger

Jakob, Out of the Village

Library and Archives Canada Cataloguing in Publication

Driedger, William, 1922-
    Jakob, out of the village / William Driedger.

ISBN 978-1-894431-13-2

    1. Old Colony Mennonites--Saskatchewan--Fiction.
I. Title.

PS8607.R425J32 2007   C813'.6   C2007-901854-8

Cover: © istockphoto.com/Jolanta Stozek

Printed in Canada
April 2007

This publication was made possible in part by a grant from the D.F. Plett Historical Research Foundation, Inc.

Your Nickel's Worth Publishing
Regina, SK.

www.yournickelsworth.com

foreword

William Driedger grew up in an Old Colony Mennonite village on the Canadian prairies during the '30s and '40s. He now lives in Regina, Saskatchewan.

William Driedger, author of *Jakob, Out of the Village*, is my older brother. With my persistent pestering, he finally completed the manuscript when he was in his early eighties.

Sadly, in the last few years it has been increasingly evident his short-term memory has become a problem. I was afraid his manuscript would never be published. I felt his writing was too valuable to let die and obtained his permission to ensure this labour of love would become a finished product. You now hold that effort in your hands.

Jack Driedger
March 2007

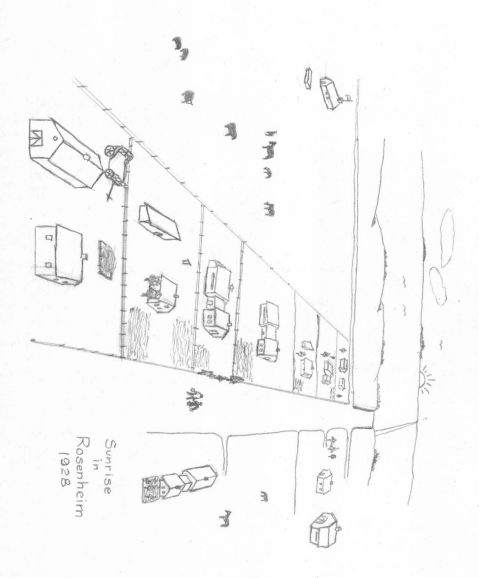

Sunrise
in
Rosenheim
1928

Glossary of Plautdietsche Words

Bengel:	rascal
Binga:	reaper, binder
Daugenix:	good-for-nothing
Donnadach:	Thursday meeting of church elders, disciplinary meeting
Faspa:	midafternoon light lunch *(see Supsil & Prips)*
Forsinger:	one who faced the congregation and led the singing in church
Gank:	connecting structure between house and barn
Gondach:	good day, a greeting
Hingst:	stallion, a horse, usually purebred, for breeding
Kjäkshe:	hired girl who helped both indoors and outdoors
Mumkje:	title of a married woman
Ohms:	church elders
Omkje:	title of a married man
Plautdietsch:	a dialect of Low German
Prips:	a brew of roasted wheat, a coffee substitute *(see Faspa)*
Schlingel:	a rogue or scoundrel; disreputable
Schlope-metz:	a slow thinker, accident-prone
Schnieawest:	laced undergarment, designed to flatten the breasts
Schusta:	shoe-repairman
Schwien schlachten:	pig butchering
Stolt:	proud or vain
Summaborscht:	summer borscht; a hearty soup of meat and vegetables
Supsil:	homemade jam *(see Faspa)*
Undertalk:	a private dialogue which could lead to discipline
Wurst:	sausage
Zodeltiet:	seeding time in spring
Zwieback:	a bread roll formed from two *(zwei)* pieces of dough

Part
one

1928 - 1944

Jakob Schellenberg doesn't know that he lives in the centre of North America on the northern edge of the Great Plains. This is where he was born and has lived his life of six years—in the farm village of Rosenheim half a mile west of the river, six miles east of town where the train stops to pick up or leave mail and take people to the city.

The Promise

THE JULY DAY HAD BEEN HOT AND HEAVY. It was early afternoon. A dark line of cloud lay on the horizon, traced by faint flickers of lightning. A murky blue lifted from the layer of cloud and swiftly covered the western sky. The air chilled the sweat-stained shirts of the man and boy who anxiously scanned the horizon.

For three years the land had been thirsty. Each spring, as the first green shoots of grain struggled up through the dry crust, hordes of hungry grasshoppers cut them down—where they were then replaced by Russian thistle which thrived in the dry, dusty soil. The farmers tried to control the insects with a bait of sawdust, bran and molasses laced with arsenic, scattered by hand paddles from horse-drawn wagons.

One farmer, careless from exhaustion and despair, forgot to close the bin in which the bait was stored. His starving cow, hungry for more than thistle, ate the bait and died. Even if there had been a telephone in the village the farmer would not have called for a veterinarian. The loss of a ten-dollar cow was more affordable than the veterinarian's fee.

This year the fields looked better than ever. One more rain would fill the kernels of wheat for a good harvest. For the first time in Jakob's memory Papa spoke of twenty-five bushels per acre.

They scanned the sky and inhaled the cool air. The dark blue wall was now overhead and covered half the sky. In the distance a sheet of gray poured straight into the ground.

"It looks like a heavy rain."

"I don't like that cold air," said Papa.

And then, a faint rushing sound.

"Inside! Quick!"

The hailstones clattered against the windows and rattled off the roof. Papa stared through the screen door as the balls of ice bounced off the ground and shrouded the farmyard in white.

One minute of destruction. Then silence. This year's crop was gone, knocked to the ground.

"Maybe next year," he sighed.

Jakob looked at Papa. His eyes looked tired.

"Why is the weather so bad?"

"The weather comes from God. He knows what is best for us."

The sun broke out, mirrored in the prisms of a thousand raindrops hanging from the maple leaves. In the east, across a blue sky, a rainbow burst into view. A bird twittered, hesitantly. Then a warble, growing to a jubilant chorus of chirps and trills.

"Mama, where does the rainbow come from?"

"The Bible says it's a promise from God that He will never again flood the world and drown every creature."

She filled the kettle and put it on the stove.

Bread

MUMKJE SCHMIDT ACROSS THE STREET was a jolly neighbour whom Mama was careful not to offend, but Papa said that she was a hardy soul with whom one could be direct. That was Papa, always direct, candid, though never cruel. People trusted him. But he was also clever.

On the day they moved into their house, Mumkje Schmidt came to the door, all a-smile.

"Will you loan me a loaf of bread? I haven't had a chance to bake yet. I will return a fresh loaf as soon as my husband gets the stovepipe connected."

Mama, as always, was delighted to be of help to a pleasant neighbour. But Papa expressed some doubt. He often asked questions that never occurred to Mama.

"What is there to be so very happy about?"

The very next day the neighbour was at the door with a freshly baked loaf of bread.

"See?" Mama smiled. "She didn't forget."

The bread was hard and tough and sour. Even the dog wouldn't eat it. And so it was dropped in the slop pail for the pigs who ate anything.

"Now what shall we say if she asks did we like her bread?" asked Mama.

After several seconds, Papa said, "We can say it was greatly relished. We don't have to say by whom." He was very scrupulous about the truth.

Several days later the neighbour, with smiling apologies, explained that unexpected guests had eaten all her bread. And Mama gave her another loaf.

"How can I stop this?"

"Let me think about it," said Papa, as he went out to feed the pigs.

Twice more Mumkje Schmidt came to borrow bread. And when she brought a loaf in exchange for the first, Mama wrapped and saved it in the cellar. The next time she came to borrow bread, Mama went to the cellar, came back and, with a smile, returned the neighbour's own bread.

The neighbour never borrowed bread again.

Mama and Papa smiled.

The Garden

ON WEEKDAYS THE MENNONITES came to the city to shop or peddle their garden produce to households. The women wore ankle-length dark skirts with long-sleeved high-buttoned blouses, loose-fitted and pleated to conceal the figure. The only decorative article of clothing was a knotted shawl, hand-embroidered with a fringed hem. They walked behind their husbands, who were mostly dressed in new overalls and a secondhand but clean suit jacket, preferably of navy blue serge, and a navy or dark brown shirt, with or without a collar and, rarely, a necktie. A tweed cap or dark felt hat topped a clean-shaven face, deeply tanned by the prairie sun and wind.

That was the only time city folks saw them unless they drove out to see the settlement of farm villages.

The first ten miles of paved highway out of the city were a pleasant drive. The next ten were gravel, dangerous to windshields and headlamps, except on Sundays when the drivers of heavy trucks had the day off. The last eight miles of dirt crumbled to dust when the summer was hot and dry. This year the weather had been good. The road was hard-packed and the fields were green.

"There's Rosenheim. Those trees were planted in 1895."

His passengers fell silent and shifted their position for a better view of the scene ahead, their attention caught by the shimmer of cottonwood leaves. Tall caragana around the first house concealed the driveway of the second until they passed the hedge to allow a splash of red, orange and yellow marigolds, poppies and nasturtiums rouse eyes that had been dulled by miles of open sky, flat horizons and waving grain fields in every direction.

Over the fence were rows of pink and white carnations and a rainbow of red, white, blue, purple and yellow sweet peas, morning glories, zinnias, petunias and snapdragons. In the background, sunflowers had turned their golden petals to face the sun.

The dark green touring car passed the driveway, slowed and came to a hesitant stop. The woman beside the driver leaned forward, pointing to the garden. Two passengers in the back seat gestured out the window.

City folk!

When the driver shifted gears and turned his head to look out the rear window as he backed up, Jakob bounded up the steps into the house.

"The *Englaenda* are coming to see the garden!"

Mama moved the pot of *Summaborscht* to the back of the range and wiped her hands on her apron. With the fluid motion of habit she stepped into her sandals, picked up a wide-brimmed straw hat and flop-flopped out the screen door, adjusting her hat as the car rolled to a stop. Jakob recognized the red triangle on the rear fender of a 1928 Chevy sedan which announced its new four-wheel brakes. The hood and fenders, headlamps and bumpers gleamed through the light film of road dust.

"Hello." The driver smiled as he swung the car door open. He half turned his body to drop his foot on the running board, his arm on the polished wooden steering wheel. "We saw—I mean ... could we look at your flowers?"

His companion leaned forward, her red lips parted, cheeks rouged and dimpled. A floppy wide-brimmed hat matched her white gloves. Jakob knew she would be wearing white shoes with elegant high heels like a Lady from the City or members of the royal family whom he'd seen in Mama's scrapbook of clippings. One of her favourite pictures was the family of the Russian czar before they were murdered by the Bolsheviks.

Mama gave a shy smile. "Come," and started for the garden gate. City folks who came to see her garden were always welcome.

The driver stepped out and walked around the car to open the door for the Lady. Jakob sidled to the right to catch a better view of her leg as she stepped onto the running board. In the light breeze he caught a whiff of perfume. As she turned in his direction he pretended to remove a sliver from the instep of his foot, balancing easily on one leg. He rolled down his pants to hide the thistle scratches and, assuming a frown of concentration, inspected a broken nail on his toe.

She bent to straighten her stockings and the front of her blouse fell forward. Under lowered eyelids, he observed her closely. In her earlobe was a single pearl earring. Her wrist, so slender and white, wore a gold-coloured bracelet with sparkling blue stones to match the ring on her finger, like the jewelry that Mama liked to look at in the city. That happened only when Papa had farm business, when he picked up repair parts from the implement dealer. When they were alone Mama took Jakob to different places to look at things they never saw with Papa. Mostly to Woolworth's and Kresge's where clerks didn't ask if they could help.

The couple in the back seat exited as well, and as they moved off he stepped close to the car. He could smell the heat of engine oil and hear the faint clicks of contracting metal through the side vents of the hood. A pair of lace-trimmed gloves were folded on the front passenger seat. Small gloves. For delicate hands. On the driver's seat lay a flat-topped straw hat, hard-brimmed. He inhaled a mix of leather, perfume and tobacco smoke. In his imagination he felt his left hand grip the polished walnut of the steering wheel, the other palm the matching gear shift knob and his right foot reach for the gas pedal.

"Jakob!" Mama called from the garden gate.

Boys shouldn't stand close to cars. People might think he would touch or take something. He lingered for a last look at the instruments in the polished wooden panel before he turned away and caught up with the visitors as they followed Mama into the garden. He latched the gate behind him.

Mama led, the ladies following. The gentlemen lagged a few paces, talking English. They made much to-do with cigarette holders, lighting, inhaling and exhaling. He was glad Papa, who had some funny ideas about smoking, wasn't there. His remarks could be offensive and embarrassing.

"If we were made for smoking we'd have chimneys sticking out of our heads."

Jakob's older brothers, Knals and Obraum, smoked—but only when they were with other big boys and Papa wasn't around.

Mama led the visitors between rows of crisp green lettuce, juicy stems of rhubarb, carrots and cabbages, onions and kohlrabi, watermelon, cantaloupe, cauliflower and cucumbers, beets and beans, potatoes and parsnips.

"Frank, look at these beautiful carnations!" exclaimed the Lady with the earring.

Mama took a knife from her skirt pocket, snapped it open and cut a bouquet of pink and white carnations for the visitor. Her companion fingered the coins in his pocket, uncertain whether or not he should offer to pay for the flowers, but relaxed when she cut a second bouquet of sweet peas for the other lady.

The visitors bent down to touch the fresh green leaves of lettuce and, hesitantly, the second lady asked if she could buy some.

Mama smiled. "You buy anything."

They pointed at cabbages, cucumbers, carrots and radishes. Mama picked up the corners of her apron and Jakob filled it with vegetables.

They returned to the car and he ran to the summer kitchen for an apple box which the driver placed on the floor behind the front seat. After stowing the vegetables he drew out his wallet and asked how much. When Mama replied they looked at each other and smiled. She folded the dollar bills and slid them in her skirt pocket with the pocketknife.

With smiles and thank-yous and goodbyes, the visitors settled in the car, started the motor and with a wave of hands drove off to tell their friends about the quaint Mennonites with the beautiful flower-and-vegetable garden in the village. Only an hour's drive from the city on a Sunday afternoon.

"Look for the tall cottonwoods. You can't miss it. The second house on the left."

4

Christmas

AT THE END OF SUMMER, after the grain was harvested and the mornings turned crisp and cold, Jakob diligently checked the village mailbox.

The people of Rosenheim shared one post office box in the nearest town served by the railway. Any villager who went to Olsen on personal business picked up all the mail in box 51 and, when he returned, put it in the village box which was nailed to the inside wall of the *Gank* that separated the Neufeld house from the barn. House, *Gank* and barn were one long building.

When the Fall and Winter catalogue came, Jakob always tried to be the first to turn the smooth paper untouched by any other human being, to smell the fresh printer's ink and look at the pages of Christmas toys.

"J" was the first letter he had learned to print and he marked all the toys and games and other things he would like to have with his initial. He would never get everything that he wished for, but it was wonderful to pretend he was rich and could have what he wanted. It was like having two Christmases. And having it in your head was almost as good as having it for real. Sometimes better, and always cheaper.

This year he marked a train set with a spring-wound locomotive, coal tender, tank car, two freight cars with sliding doors, a red caboose, an oval track, a tunnel and a railway station with a crossing signal. A dump truck. A drawing book and watercolours. A real steam engine with alcohol burner. A cowboy outfit with chaps, hat, shirt and spurs. A cap pistol with three rolls of caps. An air rifle—and a pop gun, in case he didn't get the air rifle. And skates.

He sometimes wished for a Christmas tree with candles and tinsel and glass balls and stars and an angel at the top like he saw in pictures.

But Papa said it was pagan. It wasn't right to prettify life with decorations and adornments like lipstick, jewelry, neckties and curtains.

Mama often looked at ruffled curtains in the catalogue.

In early November, Papa made his monthly shopping trip to Olsen, six miles west. Eldest brother Knals went out to hitch the two biggest horses to the bobsled. Filled with wheat for delivery to the grain elevator, it would be loaded with coal on the return trip. As Papa shrugged into his sheepskin jacket, Mama showed him a stamped envelope to Eaton's. She spoke in low tones and pulled out some dollar bills, pushed them back into the envelope and gave the envelope to him for mailing.

"Where did you get so much money?"

"From my garden." Her eyes wrinkled at the corners, like she was trying not to smile.

On Christmas Eve everyone in the family, Papa and Mama and the four brothers, Knals, Obraum, Jakob and Petah, set gray enamel bowls around the family table. Each bowl had a tag tied through a hole in the rim. That was how he learned to write his full name.

So that Christmas morning would come quicker, Jakob went to bed early. But he couldn't sleep. Once or twice he heard someone in the kitchen but when he listened hard he heard only Papa snoring and the wall clock ticking. By the dim light of the kerosene lamp he saw the shiny brass pendulum swinging ... *tick tock, tick tock*. He hoped Papa hadn't locked Santa out. In the morning he would look for sleigh tracks in the fresh snow.

He thought about the catalogue. He should have included a sled. He had mentioned it to Mama but forgot to mark it. And then the clock made the hissing noise that comes before the gong. He counted ... dong ... dong ... dong .... Mama said he could get up at six o'clock. Three more hours.

"Jakob. Wake up! It's Christmas morning."

"What time is it?" He sat up, wide awake.

"Seven o'clock."

Tossing aside the woolen quilt, he swung his legs out of bed and sprinted into the kitchen.

It was there, like the picture in the catalogue. The locomotive, freight cars, caboose, tunnel, station. He tried the sliding doors, they worked perfectly. The locomotive even had a lever to make it back up. There was also a wooden pencil box, with a painted picture of a boy and girl and a dog surrounded by red and yellow flowers. He opened the lid and found a pencil that was blue on one end and red on the other, a pen holder with a cork hand-piece and three nibs. A man-size handkerchief, red with white dots, a ruler, a colouring book and crayons. And in the bowl were peanuts, almonds and hazelnuts, an apple, an orange, two chocolate bars, two marshmallow cookies and a paper tube of red popcorn. He tore open the bottom and found the prize, a miniature Union Jack flag.

"Look under the table." Papa had entered the room.

It was a heavy sled. Jakob had never seen one like it. The runners were made of thick steel strongly riveted to brackets bolted to a solid wooden platform. Heavy and strong, the way Papa made things.

Suddenly he had to go.

"Your boots! Your coat!" Mama noticed what others didn't see and, sometimes, what others only felt.

She held his boots for his feet and as he rushed for the door, she threw his Mackinaw over his shoulders. He stepped into the chilly vestibule and his fingers stuck to the icy metal knob of the outer door. Hinges creaked with frost as he opened and closed the door behind him. The snow crunched under his boots. It was dawn, the coldest time of day on the open plains of a prairie winter. A spreading light outlined the hoarfrost on the garden fence, sparkled the snow on the roofs and whitened the plumes of vapour drifting from the village chimneys. His nostrils tightened in the frigid air and he gagged as the sharp air struck his lungs. Covering nose and mouth with his hand, he ran around the corner of the house. At the picket fence he stopped, squeezing his legs together in spasms as his numbing fingers fumbled at the buttons on his pants. Jakob sighed with relief as the bladder pressure eased and an icy yellow slot appeared in the snow, vapour rising from the stream. He kicked fresh white snow over the yellow stains and, pants unbuttoned, ran into the house, shivering.

It was after breakfast when he remembered.

"What did you get, Mama?"

She opened a shoebox. Held together with rubber bands were brightly coloured envelopes with pictures of lettuce and carrots and cabbages and poppies and marigolds and zinnias and petunias and snapdragons.

"Is that all? Just seeds?"

"It's what I wanted," she smiled, like she was thinking about something else.

5

A Death in Kronstahl

THE FARMALL ROW-CROP TRACTOR was designed to ride high and cut the roots off the weeds without damaging the young stalks of corn. The implement dealer had only one left in his inventory. Corn was not a popular crop in the settlement and he was anxious to unload the only Farmall before the season was over. When George Goertzen offered a down payment of one hundred dollars, the balance to be paid when the wheat crop came in, the dealer accepted. Better, he reasoned, to have a hundred dollars than a rusting tractor in the yard.

Papa shook his head. "Those high wheels, high axle. Easy to tip. Especially on those rolling hills. And George takes risks, too." Which Papa did not.

George's farm was on the edge of the Kronstahl hollow, a dip in the flat plain. Just as Papa feared, the accident happened on Tuesday when George disced the contours around a hillock. They found him pinned under the tractor, engine running, wheel spinning. They were told not to move the body and tractor until the police arrived, well past noon. It was a hot July and the funeral was planned for Friday. The women who bathed and dressed the corpse said George didn't smell so good. When a thunderstorm broke on Thursday, the air grew heavy with humidity and it wasn't nice to be close to George.

They were gathered around the coffin at the grave. Three men, their hands on shovels, were impatient for the pastor to finish the prayer. Overnight the face in the coffin had turned a shade of blue-green. A weeping woman, probably his wife, flicked a white handkerchief to drive off a fly that circled the face, attracted to the ooze from the nose that had once belonged to George. Jakob's stomach churned and, as the rank and rancid stench of rotting human flesh struck his nose and throat, he gasped and gagged. Mama put her hand on his shoulder and held a handkerchief over his nose and mouth.

Later, on their way home in the buggy, their muffled voices drifted behind the seat to where Jakob dangled his feet out of the box and watched grasshoppers flutter up from the road into the grass.

"They should have buried him yesterday."

"We should never have brought him."

"It's just as well he learns about life and death when he is young."

In bed, Jakob fitfully dozed between images of a green face, a circling fly, a white handkerchief and weeping eyes. Suddenly the dead man sat up in the coffin and stared at Jakob, who screamed.

"What is it? Did you have a dream?" He looked up. Mama touched his forehead.

"A man was chasing me." He didn't want to admit he was scared of the dead man lying in the coffin, with the blue-green face and a fly buzzing around his nose.

She tucked him in and he fell asleep.

6

Mr. Shepya

AFTER EASTER, EARLY IN SPRING before the snow was gone, Papa brought home a crate of chicken eggs which he arrayed on a tray in an incubator heated by a kerosene lamp. He marked one side of each egg with a pencil.

"Why do you do that? When will the chicks come out?" Jakob was eager to see them peck their way out of the shells.

"I must turn them twice a day, just as mother hen would. The mark tells me which ones I have turned. They'll hatch in exactly twenty-one days," said Papa.

Several times a day he checked a thermometer behind the glass door and adjusted the kerosene heater to keep the eggs warm, as they would be under a sitting hen.

As hatching day approached, Jakob and Petah eagerly checked the eggs for the smallest crack or hole, the first sign of a chick peck-pecking its way into the world. Soon the head of the first popped out, the shell cracked open and the chick came out, looking as if it had been drenched in the rain.

"Handle it carefully, don't squeeze or drop it." Mama gave Jakob and Petah each a chick to hold.

Within a day there were almost a hundred. Their first food came from a human hand, their first water from a pan filled by a hand that came with a human face. The first sound, besides their own, was the voice of a person and the first touch was when a hand picked it up and rubbed its soft fuzzy warmth against a cheek. They quickly learned that all good things came from a human face or hand or voice. They never forgot and when anyone came near the incubator they chirped lustily.

They must have thought Mama was their mother. When they grew feathers and they saw her in the farmyard, a hundred pullets fluttered after her, clucking chicken-talk. When she called them they converged from all directions, flapping wings that never flew, tumbling over one another to reach her hand. If they found it empty, they cocked one eye as chickens do, with a puzzled look.

After the soft down was replaced by feathers, they began to change in other ways. The heads of the roosters grew the beginnings of crowns and red wattles sprouted where a man might grow a beard. As boys do, the roosters began to play rough with each other.

"They are starting to fight to see who will be the rooster of the flock."

"What happens to the losers?"

Papa chuckled. "They don't know it, but we'll have chicken noodle soup."

So that the drinking water from the well under the kitchen would not be polluted, the pit for the outhouse was dug far from the house, close to the hen house. One day the flock of hens, under the watchful eye of the surviving rooster, was clucking and scratching for worms and other nice things directly across Jakob's path to the outhouse. Maybe the rooster was looking for a chance to show off to the hens. Maybe he saw the little boy as another rooster. He lowered his head, fluffed his neck feathers, dropped the near wing as a shield and, flashing an angry eye, began to circle Jakob with a sidestep shuffle: the rooster war dance. A fully grown Barred Rock rooster with his feathers fluffed is a frightening thing. Papa had shown Jakob a milk pail with a dent made by the spur of an angry rooster. Jakob slowly backed off until he was safely out of range and ran to the house.

But he couldn't hold out much longer. Somehow, he had to get to the outhouse. He looked for a stick and found a stout willow branch. As he approached the flock, the rooster fluffed out his feathers, dropped his wing and circled, coming ever closer. Jakob swung, caught him on the head and the rooster flopped on his side. His fierce eye dimmed and slowly closed.

For a moment Jakob forgot his urgent need and ran to the garden where Mama was hoeing.

"Mama, Mama, I killed the rooster," and he described what happened.

"Maybe it's time for chicken noodle soup. Let's have a look."

When they approached the outhouse the rooster was on his feet, staggering like a drunk. After a few minutes he looked almost normal.

"I guess the soup will have to wait," said Mama.

The rooster never threatened Jakob again. But they met once more, in winter.

Like many people, Papa liked to give surprises even more than getting them himself. In winter, when snow covered the ground, the chickens roosted in their own barn where Papa made sure they had feed and water for the night. One evening he returned from his chores with the big rooster on his arm and got him to sit on the back of a kitchen chair.

When it turns dark, roosters realize the sun has set and the day is over. When he saw the light in the kitchen, he thought it was the morning sun. He flapped his wings and crowed. And he crowed. And crowed. Everyone laughed and laughed. And laughed.

"Now that he is a member of the family, he must have a name," said Papa. "What should we call him?"

"Mister Shepya," said the youngest brother, Petah. And that's what everyone called him, which is *Plautdietsch* for Mr. Barred Rock.

Ropes and Chains

PAPA CAME HOME FROM AN AUCTION with a "new" horse, a bay gelding with white face markings. Jakob and his brothers gathered around to look him over, careful not to stand within kicking range until they got to know him better.

"He's only about five years old and I got him cheap. I hope he doesn't have any bad habits. We'll soon find out."

"What's his name?"

"The man called him Bill. We can change the name later if we want."

Knals matched him with Sandy, the biggest and most placid horse on the farm. Sandy had clever ways of managing affairs for his comfort. In midsummer, when insects harassed the horses, they were fitted with mesh nose baskets to keep insects out of their tender nostrils. When Sandy found the basket uncomfortable, he pushed his massive head against the wagon pole to bend and dislodge it. When the insects pestered him again, he had a way of pushing it back over his nose.

Knals hitched them to a heavy wagon, where the bay could do the least damage if he became hard to handle. Immediately, he nipped at Sandy, who gave him a muscular push with his massive hindquarters. This settled Bill down.

Jakob climbed up on the seat beside Knals, who turned the team around. The bay flattened his ears but didn't try to bite. On the village street Knals urged them to a trot. They quickly fell into a matching stride. After half an hour, they were unhitched, watered, fed and tethered in a double stall. If the bay should try to kick, the roan had the weight to throw him off balance against the wall.

After *Faspa*, when Jakob and Papa came out of the house, the bay was grazing in the barnyard, the tattered rope dangling from his halter.

"So that's why they sold him! We'll give him a surprise."

From a steel rod Papa made up a heavy eye-bolt and anchored it securely to the front stanchion. He made a noose from a heavy chain, looped. If the bay pulled hard it would tighten around his neck and choke him.

"He must never do that again. Not even once. We will teach him, in this barn, his old tricks won't work. We'll make the rope a little longer than the chain so the chain will tighten first. We want him to think it's the rope that is holding him. If he escapes once more we'll have to shoot him. Food for someone's mink farm."

"Couldn't we sell him? They wouldn't have to know that he breaks halters."

"That wouldn't be honest. We will try to break a bad habit and make him useful."

Almost as soon as they left the barn they heard a rasping grate as the noose tightened, followed by the thump of a body against the stall. A moment of silence. Then, a succession of noises, rasping, rattling, thumping and stomping. And silence.

"I think that will do it. But always put the chain on him and make sure it's a little shorter than the rope."

"Why don't we chain our other horses?"

"We don't need to. They are chained—in their minds. When they were young they weren't strong enough to break the rope. Now, they never try."

Part
two

1875

In 90 years the original group of 523 Mennonite families who came from Prussia to South Russia has swelled to more than 50,000. Their isolation on the steppes of Ukraine has sheltered their culture from history. The French aristocracy has been guillotined, Leo Tolstoy has written War and Peace to immortalize Napoleon's invasion and retreat, Alfred Lord Tennyson has glorified valour in "The Charge of the Light Brigade," the U.S. Civil War has cost nearly a million men (women and children not included), President Lincoln has been assassinated, Bismarck is Chancellor of the German Empire and Victoria is queen of the British Empire and Empress of India.

Catherine the Great, who granted them freedom of religion and education and exemption from military service, has been succeeded by son Paul I who was strangled by the nobles. Czar Alexander I has suffered from the armies of Napoleon and Czar Nicholas I humiliated by Turkey and its western allies. The current Czar, Alexander II, sets out to adopt western technology and culture. He frees the serfs, reduces class and ethnic privileges, attacks corruption, reorganizes the army and introduces universal military service. Russian is to be the official language of education.

Loss of privilege, fear of assimilation and a growing gap between rich and poor will drive a third of the Mennonite population out of Russia to Canada and the U.S. Four delegates have just returned from negotiations with Canadian authorities.

Out of Russia

"SO YOU'VE DECIDED? You're going?"

"Absolutely. Canada has promised everything we want ... in writing." Petah Schellenberg passed a document to his visitor. "This is an official translation of a letter from John Lowe of the Department of Agriculture in Ottawa." From a bowl on the table, he reached for a sunflower seed.

"Hmm," Paul Hiebert, a cabinet maker in his thirties, read from the letter. "'Entire exemption from military service ... exercising religious principles ... the same privilege ... to the education of their children in schools.' Our own schools, too? But isn't that what we were guaranteed by Catherine the Great? Once they get us there, how do we know if they'll keep their word?"

"Paul, they're not Russians. They come from Europe, like us. It's a Christian nation. A democracy. I think they can be trusted to keep their word."

"Why not the United States?"

"An order-in-council was passed in March setting aside eight townships for our own use." He reached for the letter. "In Canada we can set up villages just as we did in Prussia and here. Listen to this: 'Should the Mennonite settlement extend beyond the eight townships set aside by the order-in-council ... other townships will be ... reserved to meet the full requirements of Mennonite immigration.' Surely, that's as much as we can expect from any government?"

"What about Indians? We hear a lot about them scalping settlers."

"That's the States. To keep order and enforce the law in Canada, the North West Mounted Police have been set up. "

Petah Schellenberg reached for another seed. "I'm worried about

Johann. He turns seventeen next year."

"Yes. He goes in the Czar's army or the forestry. Seventeen. I'll never forget my seventeenth birthday. Like it was yesterday."

"You were in the Crimea."

Paul nodded.

"I was drafted to supply the Russians. We didn't have a wagon and team to spare. Like many others, I drove for the Niehburs to haul a load of flour to the front and bring back the wounded. They directed me to an artillery battery. After I unloaded, an officer suggested I get a night's rest before leaving in the morning so I rolled up in a blanket and lay down under the wagon. At dawn I was awakened by a lot of commotion and shouting The men were loading the big guns and stacking shells. The officer motioned for me to join him.

"'Look at those dumb Englishmen,' he shouted above the noise, 'riding straight into cannon range!' There in the valley, far below, was a troop of cavalrymen on horses. Hundreds of them. Six abreast in red uniforms and polished brass buckles and buttons, sabres flashing in the rising sun, they were a stirring sight."

"Didn't they see their danger?"

"If they had looked up either side of the valley they must have seen cannon lined up on both sides. When the last of the formation entered the valley the captain shouted 'Fire!' As the first shell exploded among the riders, the artillery across the valley opened up. When the shelling stopped the Cossacks rode in, slashing anyone who moved. It was a field of guts and blood and shit of animal and man. After I puked we loaded our sick and wounded from the previous battle and got out of there."

"The commander was probably hanged when he got home."

"Ha! An Englishman wrote a poem glorifying their bravery! Tennyson, I think, 'The Charge of the Light Brigade.'"

"Some of our people got rich on the Crimean War. Herman Niehbur sold tons of flour to the army, called it the 'golden age' of milling. The big landholders supplied the Russian army with wagons, teams and drivers to transport troops and munitions to the front. Daniel Petash made millions selling wool for uniforms. In Halbstadt, Obraum Driedja and Knals Lepp got gold watches with an inscription of gratitude from the Czar. Doft Friesen, the mayor of Molotschna, was invited to the Czar's coronation. With their profits they bought up thousands of acres of land, driving up prices. When Wellm Martens died and his widow divided their land among ten children, each one inherited 25,000 acres. Now, half of our people have no land. It's not right."

"You have to admit, the rich gave generously to build a hospital, a high school, a school for the deaf and an orphanage."

"Yes, it makes them feel good, but it humiliates the poor. I suppose that's why it's more blessed to give than to receive. But I think there's a better way. When things are done right the poor get a lift and the rich don't have all the power."

"And how could we do that?"

"We Mennonites have a lot of wealth with which we could buy land for those who have none. But on matters of money only those who have land can vote and they don't want to lose the cheap and obedient labour they get from the poor. But I'm worried about Johann. Last year he had his eye on a Russian peasant girl. This year it's the Lepp girl."

"The rich Lepps?"

"Johann doesn't know his place. The rich marry the rich and they get richer. He doesn't want to play by the rules. He doesn't fit in."

"Maybe you should send him to *Jugend Verein* on Sunday evening, to sing hymns and read the Bible with other young people like himself." [1]

"I don't want him to associate with the Brethren who are forever converting others to join their jumping, thumping, drumming and shouting in church. The Neufeldsche saw an elder smooching a young girl in the kitchen. A sister kiss, he said it was. It is unseemly. Our way of life has always been to live simply and live frugally, to keep out of war and politics. Nothing has been simple since the emperor freed the serfs. They are landless like many of us. There is no freedom without land. When night comes, they graze their cattle on the lands of Mennonites. They steal whatever they can. So, what do some of our Mennonites do? They hire Cossack guards to protect their property. And you know how brutal they are. Ostentatious living is not the way of our people. I fear what we call the golden age is another name for greed and ambition. We shall reap what we sow and I am afraid of the harvest."

"What's the name of your new village in Canada?"

"Blumenfeld."

Field-of-Flowers.

---

[1] *Jugend Verein* is a "young people's group" or "youth group," in this case referring to Church-sanctioned gatherings for older teenagers or young adults of the congregation.

Grandpa and the Church

JOHANN SCHELLENBERG WAS A TEENAGER when he arrived in the pioneer village of Blumenfeld, Manitoba, in 1876. He married in his late teens, built a home and started a family. Thirty years later he had seven sons and two daughters. Land prices went up and he moved to the area he knew as the Northwest Territories where homesteads of a hundred and sixty acres were available for a ten dollar registration fee. If the settler lived on the property for three years and made the required improvements, the land was his. The year before they arrived, the area became the province of Saskatchewan.

The Old Colony Church, of which he was a member, was an authoritarian church that strictly enforced its morality. Anyone who had ambitions in commerce or politics was subject to discipline. Members were expected to separate themselves from the world around them in both practice and appearance. Anyone who strayed risked excommunication and shunning, a practice based on scripture.

"... If he refuses to listen even to the church, treat him as a pagan ...." MATTHEW 18:17

They ignored their own history. Four hundred years earlier Menno Simons, a Roman Catholic priest, defied oppression and persecution to found the Mennonite Church.

And now Johann defied the authority of the church which had, over the centuries, lapsed into meaningless tradition. Instead of following the traditional occupation of farming, he traded in cattle and properties, bought a hotel and a number of stores. To travel quickly from enterprise to opportunity, he bought a 1912 EMF automobile. Instead of a traditional barn and house unit in a Mennonite village, he built a modern two-storey house close to town, with a verandah and polished oak floors.

Like his ancestors and thousands of other trailblazers, he upset traditional authority. Where could this lead?

The final justification for action came when, instead of settling differences through the church, he used the courts. He was excommunicated and his business boycotted. Instead of reforming, the church broke itself. If Grandpa had lived the normal life span of three score and ten he would have seen the church elders in voluntary exile and the rise of a new, revitalized church. But he died of cancer at sixty-one.

Like any big change, it claimed its casualties. The family dispersed, its intimacy was broken. His sons were divided. Most left the Old Colony church. Others joined the Conference church, a few abandoned all church affiliation. Papa, who had settled in the Old Colony farm village of Rosenheim, wanted to live in peace with his neighbours. He never wore a necktie, stopped card playing in the home and, like other parents in the village, demanded his children address elders by the plural, "ye."

Family gatherings became rare and argumentative. Yet, on the occasion of their parents' silver wedding anniversary, the older boys arranged for a family portrait. When asked to wear a necktie like everyone else, Papa declined.

"I would not be what I am."

On the following Sunday they gathered to view the photographs. Two of his younger brothers, with a reputation for mischief, conspired with the photographer to touch up Papa's portrait with a necktie. The enlarged family photograph was mounted and displayed on the dining table. Everyone watched as Papa approached the table with his hands clasped behind him, stared for a moment at the photo without expression, and turned to Mama.

"I think we should go home."

It was only with apologies and persuasion that he stayed. He took his commitments and his sense of integrity seriously. No one ever saw him wear a tie.

Jakob seldom saw his cousins who lived in towns and in the city. His family and social activity centered on village life in Rosenheim.

1919

Under the Treaty of Versailles, Germany, the loser of the war, is to give up the rich Alsace-Lorraine, all her overseas colonies and pay reparations of some $15 billion. The U.S. Senate never ratifies the Versailles Treaty or the League of Nations Covenant. President Wilson goes on a tour of the country to rouse public opinion in favour of the project. He is already quite sick, yet proceeds against the advice of his doctors and suffers a stroke from which he never fully recovers. Prohibition begins in the United States.

Adolf Hitler becomes the seventh member of the German Labour Party. Isoroku Yamamoto (the future admiral who will plan the attack on Pearl Harbor) leaves Japan to study at Harvard University in the United States. Captain John Alcock and Lieutenant Arthur Whitten Brown of Manchester, England, make the first direct, non-stop transatlantic flight—from Newfoundland to Ireland.

In Russia, under Lenin, 1,560,000 Russians starve this year. Nestor Makhno and his anarchists burn the village of Eichenfeld, massacre 80 of 300 Mennonites and rape the women and girls.

In Canada, Sir Wilfrid Laurier dies. The Canadian National Railway is incorporated. In Winnipeg, 30,000 workers put down their tools and walk off the job, seeking bargaining rights, better wages and better working conditions. A police charge kills one striker and wounds 30.

The father of Jakob (not yet born) builds a two-room house in the farm village of Rosenheim, which has expanded to six Mennonite families. Their two sons, Knals and Obraum, approach the age of compulsory attendance at the English language public school, one mile north of the village.

Knals and Obraum

PAPA TRIED TO BE ABSOLUTELY FAIR. When he bought overalls for one, he bought an identical pair for the other. On Christmas morning, after playing with his toys for an hour, Obraum, who was younger than Knals by a year, carefully examined his truck.

"Your truck is better than mine. Mine has a scratch on the bottom. See?"

"Let me look." Knals turned it over, examined it on all sides. "Let's trade, Obraum. I like yours better than mine."

"Oh no, you don't. I don't want yours." He snatched it back. "You always try to spoil my Christmas." Knals laughed.

One day Papa brought home a chocolate bar to share between the boys. Mama gave Knals a kitchen knife. "You cut it in down the middle and let Obraum choose the half he wants." Obraum compared the two pieces carefully, turning them over and over, decided on one, changed his mind and took the other. Each boy promptly bit into his candy, Knals nibbling little bites, his brother chomping large chunks. Obraum stopped chewing and stared at Knals' bar.

"Knals' bar is bigger than mine."

Knals laughed. "Because you picked the small bar. I got the big one."

Obraum's overalls always seemed to have accidents. As he ran by the barn, they caught on a nail that no one had noticed before. He managed to lean against the stationary engine exactly where the oil leaked from the crankcase. Although he learned to walk only a month after Knals, he mostly crawled when he played. In a few days his bare and scarred knees emerged from the frayed holes of his new overalls.

Mama patched. And patched. And patched.

"I think Obraum needs new overalls again."

Papa returned from town with two new pairs. One for Obraum, one for Knals, who said he didn't need them but Papa said it was only fair.

A few months went by. "I think Obraum needs new overalls."

"I don't need any," said the oldest.

"That's right," said Mama. "Knals has three pairs which are almost like new. He outgrew two pairs before they had any holes anywhere."

"Give them to Obraum," said Knals, "I don't need them."

Each year the Schellenbergs killed four pigs. The women were scraping the lining from the intestines which had been turned inside out and scalded for sausage-making. Mumkje Peters, looked around the room and leaned over to the ear of Mumkje Schmidt.

In a low voice. "Have you noticed the two boys? How different they are!"

"In what way?"

"Knals is so neat, so tidy. And the younger so sloppy, almost in tatters."

"Oh. You don't know?"

"Know what?"

"Young Obraum told my Diedrich that his older brother always gets new clothes and he gets Knals' castoffs."

"How unfair!"

Teacher Toews

HE DIDN'T OWN ANY LAND and needed a place to live with his wife and six children. The village elders checked his history of moral behaviour, his knowledge of the Bible, reading, writing and arithmetic, and hired him. As teacher, he and his family lived in two rooms in back of the school which, on Sundays, served as a church if a pastor was available from another church. Coal for heating and cooking was provided by the villagers.

One Sunday, Teacher Toews and his wife came to *Faspa*. Knals and Obraum were playing rummy in the kitchen and Mama asked them to take their cards and play in the attic so she could set the table.

Papa and Teacher Toews had just sat down in the parlour when the teacher asked, "You let your boys play cards?"

"Why, yes. In our home we all played rummy and other card games."

"Of course. Your father, Johann. Wasn't he excommunicated for sinning against the church?"

Papa said nothing.

"I also heard your boys calling you 'you,' instead of 'ye' as is the custom among our people. I think it very unseemly that anyone who calls himself an Old Colony Mennonite would permit such behaviour in his house."

After they left, Papa and Mama talked alone in the parlour for a long time after which he called Knals and Obraum.

"Give me the cards. Now sit down and we must talk."

He said that card playing was wrong and asked Mama to throw them in the kitchen range to burn. And they must always address Mama and Papa and older people and, especially, Teacher Toews, as "ye."

Katrina

On a spring day, one year after moving to Rosenheim when the first robin chirped a greeting from the branch of a newly planted cherry tree, Katrina was born.

"What are you looking at?" asked Papa as Mama paused at a page of the Eaton's catalogue on a Sunday afternoon.

"This cotton print would make a lovely dress for Katrina. It's only twelve cents a yard. But with all the work this summer, planting and hoeing the garden, milking cows, baking—so much to do, I won't have time to sew. Do you think, maybe some day, we can afford a Singer sewing machine?"

"Do Eaton's have them?"

"Yes. But they cost fifteen dollars."

The following week a stranger drove his buggy on the farmyard, a four-wheeled democrat from which the rear seat had been removed for something covered by a blanket. Papa greeted him as if he were expected. It was the Singer man. They lifted out the fine oak cabinet of a new Singer sewing machine and carried it into the house. The man showed Mama how to wind the thread from spool to bobbin, how to sew button holes and how to look after it.

"Where would you like it?"

They set it against the wall, under the picture of Jesus with a cluster of children, his hand on the head of a little girl and a quotation from the Bible in the shape of a rainbow: "Suffer Little Children to Come Unto Me." There it stood beside her bed between the two windows where she could look out on the cherry and plum trees, the gooseberry and currant bushes she had planted just two years ago.

That summer, when they took the train to the city, she bought a small gold-coloured locket and chain for Katrina at Woolworth's for twenty-five cents, to wear, when she was old enough, with the dress Mama planned to make that winter. At Kresge's she found a lace design that would make a pretty edging for the skirt.

In October, when the yellow leaves drifted to the ground, Katrina became fretful. One morning she was wet with perspiration. Two weeks later the only daughter Mama would nurse was buried in the village graveyard. The doctor said it was lung infection.

All winter Mama sat in her rocker by the heater and shed silent tears. Papa, in his favourite chair beside the roll-top desk, mostly stared into space. Together they read the Bible.

The Lord is my shepherd, I shall not want ... He restores my soul ... though I walk through the valley of the shadow of death ... I fear no evil for I know You are with me ... Your rod and Your staff comfort me ... surely goodness and mercy shall follow me all the days of my life ... and I will dwell in the house of the Lord forever....

"Where we will meet and be with little Katrina, forever," said Papa.

Suffer little children to come unto Me, of such is the kingdom of Heaven.

"How good it is that she was never tempted by the evil of this world, that she left it in childhood innocence to be with God," responded Mama.

I know Lord, your judgments are right ... that You have in faithfulness afflicted me ... let, I pray, Your merciful kindness be for my comfort according to Your Word, to Your servant ... Let Your tender mercies come to me ... childhood and youth are vanity. They have provoked Me to anger with their vanities.

She felt a twinge of unease. "Is God angry with me? Is He punishing me?"

How long will you love vanity? ... the Lord knows the thoughts of man ... his days are as a shadow that passes away ... walk not ... in the vanity of their mind ... vanity of vanities, all is vanity ... as it happened to the fool, so it happened to me ... vanity ... a great evil ... a sore travail ... an evil disease ... turn from these vanities to the living God ....

Was it vanity? The pretty dresses she wanted to make? The chain and locket? Was her child taken away because she wanted to make her beautiful? Was it all sin and vanity? Was God a jealous God? But Jesus loved children.

I confess my iniquity ... I am sorry for my sins. The redeemed of the Lord ... shall obtain gladness and joy ... sorrow and mourning shall flee away ... My sorrow is continually before me ... When will you comfort me? Rachel, weeping, refused to be comforted for her children were not. Thus said the Lord, refrain your voice from weeping and your eyes from tears. Your work shall be rewarded .... Remove sorrow from your heart .... Blessed are they that mourn for they shall be comforted ... your sorrow will be turned to joy. I am He that comforts you.

The winter of sorrow ended, the snow disappeared, the robin returned to chirp in the cherry tree. Mama planted a row of bulbs along the east side of the house where they would catch the early morning sun.

In the third spring after Katrina's death, when the tulips opened their red and yellow petals to the first rays of dawn, a third son, Jakob, was born into the love of her still-grieving heart.

1922

At least fifty-one American Negroes are lynched this year. Alexander Graham Bell, inventor of the telephone, dies. The first portable radio and first car radio are manufactured. The U.S. Supreme Court rules that Asian immigrants are not eligible for naturalization. Albert Einstein is awarded the Nobel Prize in physics. The tomb of King Tutankhamun (1336-1327 BC) one of the best-known rulers of ancient Egypt, is discovered. The League of Nations issues the Palestine Mandate for the establishment of a homeland for the Jewish people. The king of Italy asks Benito Mussolini, leader of the Italian Fascisti, to form a cabinet and assume power. Gandhi is arrested in India for civil disobedience and imprisoned for six years.

In the Russian famine, 300 Molotschna Mennonites starve to death. The Mennonite Central Committee starts a relief program and, by June, 25,000 in 60 villages are fed every day.

On March 1, Jakob is born. Before he can think or understand he feels the rhythm of her heart, the comfort of her breast, the taste of her milk, the sound of her voice.

13

On the Roof

A LONG AND LOW BARN shelters nine horses and four cows and, in spring, one or two calves. The walls are thin. To keep out the chill of winter, a straw-filled cribbing of willows and poplar shelters the north side. The building was to be used until there was money to build a hip-roofed barn, abutting the north end of the house. That had been two generations ago.

On a still winter night the full moon illuminated a million sparkling diamonds in the snow. Now the Northern Lights, skirts a-rustling, began their dance on the horizon, reaching up overhead as the eternal stars blinked and twinkled to a whispering rhythm.

In the summer sun, the roof became the theatre of the universe at play. In each direction as far as he can see, there's open sky. A single cloud scudded across the blue from west to east. Now two layers of clouds emerged overhead, one moving faster than the other. The patterns shifted and changed. Ghostly faces of villagers turned into dragon heads which stretched and reshaped, shrunk and divided into multiple images, then merged into new forms.

A solid layer of dark blue rose rapidly on the western horizon, veiling flickers of lightning. Swallows dipped, swooping up under the sheltering eaves.

Papa rejected lightning rods. They might challenge God.

At midnight the long summer day yielded, at last, to night ... the Big Dipper pointed to the North Star, sharp under the blue-black dome.

If you ever get lost you can always find North.

A star broke loose to streak across the sky. Had it vanished? Stopped at another place, perhaps to streak for another generation? Does anything vanish?

A bark in the distance. A dog. He inhaled deeply to send his coyote howl.

Woe-woe-woe-wahooo-ooooo-oooo-woe-woe

No answer. Perhaps the coyote listened, waiting for another to be sure. He tried again.

Woe-woe-woe-wahooo-ooooo-oooo

The dog barked. A short howl—only a dog.

Then, in the distance, a coyote ....

Woe-woe-wahooo-ooooo

Raucous barking and howling from a chorus of village dogs. More coyotes in the distance. The evening performance had begun.

1929

Over 10 years have passed since the Great War of 1914-18. Near the end, Canadians shared in the triumphant Battle of Cambrai, a three-week battle in which 7,000 Germans were captured at a cost of 44,000 Allied soldiers killed and wounded. Of 60,000 Canadian soldiers killed in the war, the dismembered bodies, limbs and tattered uniforms of 11,000 were never identified. The Great War took the lives of 8 million men in uniform and 13 million civilians. The Spanish influenza that followed took another 22 million.

In four years of war, feelings in Canada ran high. Any Mennonite caught with a copy of his church newspaper in German could be fined up to $5,000 and a possible term in prison. Fifty Mennonites were prosecuted by the Saskatchewan government for sending their children to their own schools instead of English public schools. Eleven who refused or were unable to pay were jailed. The police seized and sold their farm horses, cows and pigs at auction to pay their fines.

After the war, the government passed an order-in-council which closed the doors to Doukhobors, Hutterites and Mennonites fleeing from the Bolsheviks, who had executed their own czar, the empress and their five children.

When the order-in-council was later repealed, the first of 21,000 Mennonite refugees came from Russia, sponsored by the Mennonites who had migrated a generation earlier, before the revolution.

The year is 1929 and Jakob, the grandson of Johann, is seven.

14

The Windmill

ONE SUMMER SUNDAY they set out in the buggy, pulled by Gin, the white mare, to Reinland to visit Papa's cousin, Bishop Loeppky. Petah, up front with Mama and Papa, grasped the reins that hung from Papa's hand and pretended he was driving. Mama sat quietly with her thoughts, her calloused hand gripping the armrest whenever the buggy swayed or thumped over a stone. Jakob faced backwards, his legs dangling from the buggy from where he observed the road unwind and shrink to disappear on the horizon. Sometimes, but not very often, the voice of Papa or Mama drifted to his ears. The voice of Mama:

"I hope Knals and Obraum don't fight while we're away."

After a long while Papa answered.

"Yes, I wonder what they do when we're gone."

The shadow of the fenceposts had moved another hour when Papa spoke.

"There's Reinland. That windmill is on the Loeppky farm."

The buggy passed the first four houses and turned into a lane that separated the Loeppkys from their neighbours, where a boy of Jakob's age was playing with a stick and ring.

"That's Bernard, the Harder boy." Mama always thought of these things. "Maybe you want to go over and say hello."

Jakob and his new friend compared slingshots and found a tin can on the village street. Bernard's stone struck the ground and scattered dirt over the can.

"Watch out for the big boys. If they catch us, they will beat us up."

"Why? The big boys in Rosenheim don't hurt little boys. And if anyone did, the fathers would get together and fix him."

"Because they're mean. Look! Here they come! Run!"

There were four, in their mid-teens. The biggest looked to be the size of Knals. When they saw that Jakob didn't run, they slowed to a walk. The biggest boy grabbed Jakob by the shoulder and swung him around, face-to-face.

"Why don't you run?"

"Because you won't hurt me." Jakob was not so sure.

"Let me handle him," said one of the others. "I want to see him cry."

"I'll do it." The big one seemed to be the leader. "What makes you think I won't wop you?"

"I'll tell Papa."

"And then what?"

"He'll tell your Papa."

"And then?"

The others laughed but stopped when the big boy glared.

"You'll see." Jakob couldn't think what else to say.

The big boy looked at the ground and shuffled his feet. He kicked up the dust.

"Beat it, you little shit! I'll let you go this time."

Running as fast as he could, Jakob joined his companion at the end of the village street where he had stopped to watch.

"They didn't hurt you?" The boy stared, mouth open. "What happened?"

After *Faspa* they met again.

"Let's climb the windmill." Bernard trotted to the barn, Jakob following. The windmill was higher than the barn, even higher than the maple trees at home.

"Bend down. I'll get on your back and grab the ladder."

From the ladder the boy reached down to help Jakob.

"When you climb don't look down, it will make you dizzy."

He'd never seen the roof of a barn as a bird sees it. The trees looked different too. The leaves looked bigger, the trunk smaller. From the top the dog looked funny, waddling as it walked.

"My stomach feels sick."

"Jakob, don't look down."

They were at the top of the windmill now, where Bernard climbed through a hole in the platform.

"Okay, watch me." He swung lightly from the ladder to the platform and sat, legs dangling in the air. "Come on, I'll help you." He held out a hand.

Jakob's fingers tightened on the ladder.

"I can't." His voice quavered. "I'm scared."

A strange voice, far away. "What you boys doing?"

The four big boys, far below, so small, looking up. Then the barn and the house and the boys and everything began to spin and Jakob's stomach was churning.

"He's scared," Bernard shouted from the platform.

"Stay where you are." The big boy swung up the first rung of the ladder. "Don't look down. I'm coming."

And soon Jakob heard a reassuring voice, close and just below. "I'm here. I'll get behind you." A strong hand reached out to touch his own. His fingers relaxed.

"Everything's all right now. I'll grab your foot and place it on the next rung down."

One step at a time they climbed down, together. As Jakob touched the last rung the big boy swung him off the ladder. He staggered to recover his balance.

A not-so-big boy laughed. "I bet you shit your pants."

The big boy stepped close and rapped him on the chest. "If you aren't out that gate when I count to ten we'll see who's shittin' pants. One ... two— " The not-so-big boy was out and across the village street before the count of five.

The big boy helped him hitch old Gin to the buggy and, as they waited for Papa and Mama to say their goodbyes—which always took a long time—he turned to Jakob, with lowered voice. "Tell Knals I couldn't come today, but next time I'll be there."

Jakob and Mama were alone in the kitchen. She pointed to the nickel trim along the bottom of the stove which she kept to a mirror polish.

"I wiped it yesterday. It was dusty when we came home. Fine red dust, the colour of the floor." The ladle in the soup stopped a moment.

"They were dancing here when we were gone. We won't tell Papa. It would only upset him."

The ladle moved again. In circles.

15

"Where would I go?"

PAPA WAS A CAUTIOUS AND FRUGAL MAN. Most touring cars were fitted with side curtains which a driver could button down or roll up. Would the glass windows of the new Model T Ford always work? What if it rained and the windows didn't roll up?

Waiting for a year turned out to be a wise choice. When the first Model A with the new gearshift came from the factory, he bought the dealer's last Model T at a discount. For Papa, replacing side curtains with glass windows was daring enough. To double the risk with a different gearshift was a gamble that a prudent man would avoid. He was very pleased with his 1927 Tudor.

"Why don't we go there in the car?" asked Jakob. It would be a two-hour return trip with a horse and buggy to the place where Mama's family would gather this Sunday.

"If we go by horse and buggy we'll save money," replied Papa.

"Why did we buy the car?"

"When we travel a long distance. To go to the city with a buggy for a doctor or an auction sale takes most of a day. And we would have to stay overnight. But we can get to Uncle Hendrick's in only one hour. Horses eat anyway, whether they work or stay home. The Ford would cost money for doing something that Nell will do for nothing."

If I had a car, thought Jakob, I would go by car. Always. Anywhere.

On Sunday when they arrived, three buggies, a wagon and an old Model T and Grandpa's touring car—curtains rolled up—were parked on the yard. Soon all the uncles and aunts and cousins were there. And Grandpa. But no Grandma.

Grandma was always with Grandpa. Wherever he was, she went.

Just like Mama and all the other Mamas that Jakob knew. They stayed with their Papas until one of them died.

His cousins were talking, whispering. Grandpa and Grandma had started out in the touring car. They argued on the way. Grandpa stopped the car, Grandma got out and walked away. Nobody knew where she was.

At family gatherings there was usually much chatter, laughter and sometimes hooting. Especially when they sat at table. Now, at *Faspa*, the tinkle of cups and the rattle of dishes was louder than the voices.

After *Faspa*, Grandpa left early, followed by Uncle John in his own Model T. He came back and said that Grandma was home and they were both all right.

Going home in the buggy, Mama and Papa didn't talk or laugh much. After herding the cows into the paddock to be milked, Jakob went to bed early. But he tossed in his sleep and awoke in the middle of the night, shivering, his blanket on the floor. Mama got out of bed and tucked him in.

"Mama, will you ever go away?"

"No." She paused. "Where would I go? This is home."

He curled up and fell asleep.

16

Leesa

WHEN THE BANDITS RODE DOWN from the hills of Chihuahua to plunder and pillage the Mennonite settlement, Leesa's family fled Mexico. Fearing the raiders might violate their youngest daughter, the family returned to Canada and bought a farm next to Rosenheim. Although the yields were modest, with careful management and a frugal life they successfully survived the harsh '30s.

Mama looked forward to visits from the Raleigh and the Watkins salesmen who came with their spices, liniments and other household remedies and supplies. Especially the Watkins man whose vanilla, she said, was the very best.

"He dresses nice, too."

Each housewife tried to put aside a little money to keep them coming back. Money was difficult to save and if the Watkins man was unlucky enough to come a week after the Raleigh man, he sold very little.

Leesa was fourteen when the Raleigh man came to the village that summer. Like any father in the village, Leesa's was vigilant and determined not to have a mixed marriage in his family. When she told her mother, who told Leesa's father, that she had been afraid to accept the Raleigh man's invitation to ride in his shiny car, the unlucky salesman suddenly found the doors in all the villages closed. The man from Watkins prospered.

A few months later, when Leesa's mother, who always knew of these things before he did, told Leesa's father that Ben Gerbrandt had been seen walking the village street with Leesa on a Sunday evening, he shrugged. Ben wasn't much, but he was better than an *Englaenda* or *Russlaenda*.

The formal betrothal was celebrated in Leesa's home on Saturday in midsummer, between seeding and harvest. Relatives and friends of the young couple gathered to sing hymns and to talk and to snack on roasted sunflower seeds. A *Faspa* of buns, sugar cubes and *Prips*, a brew of roasted wheat kernels, was served. When night came, the groom, who would be married in church the week after the following Sunday, slept in a separate room at the bride's home.

Next morning, her father's prized gelding—brushed until its coat shone in the sunlight, tail braided and tied with a red ribbon—was hitched to the family buggy which smelled of fresh black paint. The groom snapped the whip and the gelding stepped smartly out to take the young couple for a week of visiting relatives in the villages of the settlement. As the many *Faspas* took effect, they made frequent relief stops at willow and poplar bushes along the road.

On the following Sunday, after a simple wedding in church, the couple moved into a room in the bride's home. Before harvest, Leesa was pregnant. After threshing and before the first snow, an old granary was moved to a stony quarter section of willow and wolf berry brush. Ben tried to dig a well between the house and the sagging barn. The pick bounced off a solid layer of rock. He flung the tool to the ground and ambled to the barn where he loaded two barrels on a stone boat, hitched a horse and trudged the mile to a neighbour who had offered water from his well. It would be his weekly chore, winter and summer.

By spring, after the snow melted, Ben had stirred enough rocks with pick and shovel for Leesa to plant a small garden of potatoes, beans, peas, carrots, cabbages and sunflowers. Three years later the "Stony Gerbrandts" had two horses, a corresponding number of toddlers, four scrawny cows and a collection of turkeys, hens, pigs, geese and chickens.

"What's loose with your arm?" [2]

Leesa and Ben were having *Faspa* with her parents on a summer Sunday.

"Nothing. I banged it against the door. An accident."

"Your eye, too?" Mama could be persistent.

Her father glanced at Ben, absorbed in spreading gooseberry *Supsil* on a slice of bread, stroking it evenly with the table knife, to the edge, to the crust.

[2] In High German, *was ist los?* means "what's wrong?"

When Leesa went to the outhouse Papa looked sharply at Ben. "Don't hurt Leesa. If you do, I'll hold with you *Undertalk*."

"How is your Leesa's shoulder?"

It was Mr. Loeppky, the bonesetter, from Neuhorst. Several hundred people from the surrounding villages had come to the auction of household goods, tools, equipment and implements. The owners had sold their land and were moving to Peace River where their sons had taken up homesteads as their father had done forty years before.

"What do you mean? What happened?"

"Oh, she didn't tell you? I guess she didn't want to worry you. Yes, she sprained her shoulder. She tripped and fell."

Leesa was returning to the house with the pail of eggs when the buggy rolled on the yard. Her Papa and her elder brother were in the seat. Her youngest brother, the big one, sat in the back, his long legs dangling over the edge. In his right hand, across his knee, he held a piece of heavy machine belting, the length of his arm and the width of his wrist.

"Where's Ben?"

"Inside, Papa. Please don't hurt him."

"We only want to do this once. Tell him we want with him to *Undertalk*."

Leesa hurried into the house. At last Ben came as far as the doorway.

"Come with us to the barn."

"I don't want to," he pleaded.

"Come," said Leesa's papa, turning on his heel. Ben and his brothers-in-law followed and closed the barn door behind them.

On the following Sunday the buggy rolled to a stop, this time with only Leesa's Papa and Mama. Ben held out his hand to help mother-in-law step down.

"Leesa and I will visit while you and Papa look at the crops," she said.

Ben eased carefully into the seat beside his father-in-law.

"Your arse still hurt?"

"Better, Papa. But I can sit now. Where're we going?"

"I was in Haugh on Wednesday to have the miller grind a couple sacks of wheat. There's a bag of flour under the seat for you and Leesa. Ran into the bank manager who has a quarter of land for sale for the taxes owing: three hundred and seventy dollars. I paid fifty down. At ten or fifteen bushels of wheat an acre you can pay it off in five or six years. The house needs a new roof but my boys will help you fix the house for winter. It has a good well. No stones, either. My daughter won't be the 'Stony Gerbrandtshe' any more. Let's have a look at the place. "

He urged the mare to a brisk trot.

Crime and Punishment

"IF EVERYBODY WERE LIKE Fritz Warkentin we wouldn't have any wars." The opinions of Omkje Wieler who ran the general store in town were remembered and widely quoted, sometimes for their insight, more often for their wit.

Fritz had hired out as a farmhand to an *Englaenda* and was now in jail. Because times were hard, he wanted to earn a bit of money to pay for flour, sugar, salt and for coal to heat his mother's house in winter. One day, in a rage, his employer threw a pitchfork at a purebred Holstein cow. The veterinarian was unable to save the animal. The farmer, perhaps to recover his loss with an insurance claim, accused Fritz. The bewildered youth, tongue-tied in the presence of authority, was sentenced to a month at hard labour in prison. No one in the village knew anyone who had ever been in jail.

"What was it like, Fritz?"

"How did they treat you?"

Fritz was a heavy man who plodded as if he were walking uphill. He looked at the ground, shuffled his feet. With his sleeve, he wiped a drop of saliva from a drooping lip. And smiled.

"They were nice."

"What was jail like. Like a cage?"

"It's the first time I had my own room. I had a bed, a little table, a chair. Electric lights, too. But I got into trouble the first day. I got everybody mad. It wasn't my fault. How could I know?"

"What happened?"

"After we finished work and supper we all went to our rooms. I needed a shit. I yelled for the guards to let me out. Nobody answered. I yelled, I hollered, I banged on the door but no one came. I found some magazines. I put them in a corner and shit on them. Oh, it stunk! The smell was all over everywhere, in the other cells, too."

"What happened then?"

"You never heard such yelling. I think the guards thought there was a revolution. Five guards came running. Were they ever mad! Then they showed me what the thing in the corner was for. I thought it was for washing feet. Anyway, he made me dump the shit in the water and showed me how to pull down the little handle to make it disappear. Just like that. It gurgled and down it went. I never saw anything like that before."

"What happened after that?"

He shuffled, looked down, smiled.

"They were funny. They gave me a new name, called me Stinky. "

He paused, looking around for appreciation. It wouldn't do to make him feel too important.

"Every week they gave me clean overalls and shirt. We worked only eight hours a day and got fifteen cents an hour. Saved it for me until I went home. The food was real good, better than I ever got at home. It was a nice place. Everything so clean, too. At the end of two weeks they told me I could leave, but I said no, I wanted to stay for the month."

The villagers had never listened to Fritz before. Now he could talk about things that nobody else knew. How to crack a safe, how to get into a house when you forgot your key, although nobody in the village locked their doors. He showed the boys how he could take away a knife from somebody who tried to hurt him.

"Why would anybody want to hurt you?"

Before they went home he gave back the wallets and combs he took out of their pockets when they weren't looking.

"You sure learned a lot, didn't you?"

"It was a nice place."

In 1929, two Rosenheim families joined the Mennonite exodus to Mexico to escape public school education and other intrusions of the *Englaenda*. On this day, when all the household items, farm implements and livestock of one family were to be sold, nearly everyone in Rosenheim was at the auction.

When he saw a group of boys and men gathered around a Model T with the top down, Jakob knew it would be the salesman who had candy and apples and gum.

"C'mon, Abe. Let's see what he has." Abe was five, two years younger than Jakob. In the back seat and on a table beside the Ford was a tempting display of candy, chocolate bars, cookies, chewing gum and candy for sale.

"How much is the chewing gum?"

"Five cents for a package of five sticks."

"Let's see if we can find our parents. Maybe they will give us some money."

A crowd surrounded the auctioneer, where their parents would likely be. But neither boy saw either parent.

"All we need is ten cents. Then we could each buy a package of gum."

"I know where we can get some money," said Abe.

"Where?"

"In our parlour. There's a corner cupboard with a tin can full of money. If you can reach it we can each buy gum."

They ran across the street to the Neufeld house. No one was home.

"My sisters will be hoeing the garden. My brothers are probably in the field."

They entered the *Gank* and went through the family kitchen into the parlour. Abe pointed to a tobacco can on the top shelf of the red corner cupboard.

"Can you reach it?"

Standing on a chair, Jakob saw that the tin was nearly full of coins. He took two nickels, climbed down and gave one to Abe, and they skipped across the street back to the Model T.

"Where did you get the money?" the driver asked.

"From a tobacco tin at my house," said Abe.

He laughed and turned to the big boys hanging around the Model T. "They stole the money." They laughed and said Jakob and Abe would get into trouble.

When Jakob came home Papa asked if they had stolen money.

"No, I never steal anything from anyone. We took it because it was there."

Papa looked surprised. "Try to remember," he said, "anything that doesn't belong to you, belongs to someone else."

Later, when he went to school, Jakob discovered that two boys brushed their teeth with toothpaste instead of baking soda. An advertisement in *The Country Guide* promised a free sample of Pepsodent toothpaste for "ten cents to cover postage and handling," which he didn't have. Nor did he have a postage stamp to mail the coupon.

He cut out the coupon and each day looked through the waste basket at Papa's roll-top desk for discarded envelopes until he found a postage stamp almost perfect, with hardly a trace of the postmaster's cancellation. With a kitchen knife, he carefully scraped it clean and glued it to an envelope he had made from notebook paper. He inserted the coupon which said "I enclose ten cents ...." and cut a slot a little bigger than a dime in the bottom of the envelope.

He mailed it and, every day, checked the mailbox at the Neufeld's. Whenever a strange automobile drove through the village he was a little anxious. Had the inspectors seen the stamp? Was it a Mountie looking for him?

When it came he used it very sparingly and it lasted many months. But each morning as he brushed his teeth he had uneasy thoughts about the Royal Mail inspectors and the Mounties. When the toothpaste tube was empty he buried it in the cow pasture and skipped home.

He was happy to be free of it.

The Stick

THE SEASONS WERE CAPRICIOUS, relentless, unforgiving. If the kernels of grain were planted too soon, the young shoots could be killed by an early frost. The rains were unpredictable. If early or late, they punished or rewarded at random the deserving and undeserving, the lazy and the diligent. If the fields escaped hail and grasshoppers, an early autumn frost might kill the kernels before they filled and ripened.

Knals was sixteen, Obraum fifteen and both were out of school. At the age of six, the boys had been able to control a team of horses without danger of runaways. At fifteen, they could harness and hitch a team of four horses to harrows, a plow, a discer, a seeder or reaper and pick up a hundred-pound sack of wheat and hoist it to a shoulder.

Papa could now attend to the many chores: repairing fences, hauling manure, helping Mama milk the four cows, feeding four hogs, sharpening plowshares, replacing the cutting knives and adjusting the knotter on the reaper so it would be ready to harvest the grain. If he needed anything from town he hitched light-footed Nell to the buggy. The mare was also a spare workhorse if one of the other eight turned sick or developed collar sores. A chafing collar could disable a horse and Papa regularly examined the shoulders of each horse when they came home from the field. The family's survival depended on his attention to many things.

Now it was *Zodeltiet* and seeding was under way. One team of four, driven by Obraum, pulled the harrows to break up the clods of earth. Knals drove the team that pulled the seed drill. After each one-mile lap around the field, he refilled the drill box with seed grain from a wagon.

Gulls appeared from nowhere. They hovered over the work teams, motionless, then suddenly dipped down to pull a worm from the upturned soil. Collie, the cattle dog, followed the spoor of gophers, badgers, stoats and skunks. His nose to the ground, he was unaware of the brooding prairie partridge until he was upon the nest. The hen fluttered at ground level, feigning injury, the dog in pursuit. Safely away from the nest, the bird suddenly took wing and soared, leaving the dog mystified.

At the end of the ten-hour day, the two teams were unhitched from the implements and two horses were hitched to the wagon, now nearly empty of seed grain. The other six were tethered on each side. An hour later, the wagon, the two boys and eight horses drove onto the farmyard. By seven o'clock the animals were unhitched, unharnessed and in the barn, watered and fed.

"Knals. Where are you going? "

In the busy season when everyone was up before six to feed and water the horses and milk the cows, Papa insisted that every member of the family be in the house by ten o'clock. Although it was nine o'clock, the summer sun barely touched the horizon.

"To see the fellows."

"You were late yesterday. I want you home by ten."

Knals said nothing as he walked out the screen door.

After ten, with no sign of his elder son, Papa went to the woodpile and returned with a heavy willow stick which he leaned against the corner of the room.

"Are you going to hit him with that?" Mama was alarmed.

Papa said nothing.

An hour later Knals came in and, without a word or glance at anyone, strode up the stairs. Papa picked up the stick.

"No, no, don't," said Mama.

Papa slowly walked up the steps. Mama's face was paler than Jakob had ever seen it. They sat, silent, listening. Jakob heard conversation but couldn't understand the words.

Then a thump of boots, scraping and scuffling.

Mama cringed.

Knals shouted words that he used only when he lost his temper with big Mike, the black gelding with the flying mane. And only if Papa wasn't around to hear him.

Mama held her head, hands over her ears. Her eyes were shut. A tear slid down her cheek.

Silence.

It seemed a long time before Papa came down the steps. His hands were empty. Shoulders slumped, he shuffled into the parlour and closed the door. In a little while Mama wiped her eyes and followed.

The sun set, spreading a border of rosy sky on the western horizon. The house was quiet. Jakob sat on the porch, his hand on the dog. Collie leaned close, touching him. To the east a wisp of cloud floated over the moon. A star shot an arc across the blue and died.

He heard the screen door.

"Come to bed, Jakob," she whispered. "It's late."

She tucked him in and he fell asleep.

A big gray bear came out from behind the barn to attack him. His legs were heavy and he couldn't run. As the bear came closer, its face was Papa and he had a stick in his hand.

"Mama! Mama!"

A hand touched his shoulder.

"What is it, Jakob?"

"A big man was chasing me with a stick and I couldn't run."

"You had a bad dream. Go back to sleep." She folded and tucked the quilt under his feet. He felt warm and safe inside. "He won't do it any more."

And he didn't.

19

Unkel Franz and Maria

WHEN GRANDPA DIED of stomach cancer, Papa's younger brother Franz took over the family farm. He was a quiet man with a gentle smile. When the two brothers were together, they understood much more than they said. Long minutes of silence between words were separated by quiet chuckles.

When Unkel Franz passed his mid-twenties, Grandma quietly expressed concern about her shy son. If he stayed unmarried until thirty, he would probably never have anyone to cook for him, keep house or wash and iron his Sunday shirts. And who would want to visit him or invite him to weddings or pig butchering if he didn't have a wife?

Back in Russia, Maria was eleven, the oldest of four children, when she lost both parents in ten days, one to tuberculosis and the other to the 1917 influenza epidemic. Now, at eighteen, she and her younger brother were on a boat from Odessa to Liverpool where they would board an ocean liner to Canada. Little Jasch was ill and she was anxious to get to Canada. Aboard ship, Maria met and fell in love with Klaus, a Mennonite youth about her own age who was also fleeing Russia for Canada. They pledged to marry as soon as they could.

In Liverpool, the customs inspector looked at her brother and called another official who said the illness was infectious and they would be quarantined for at least a week. And so the two lovers were separated but promised to be faithful until they found each other again.

A week later Maria and Jasch continued their journey to Canada on another ship.

Unkel Franz had turned his cup upside down in the saucer as a sign that he had finished coffee when Grandma said, "Franz, I need a young woman to help with the milking and the garden. Another group of Mennonite refugees has arrived from Russia at the shelter. Until they find work they will need a place to call home. Will you go and look for a strong girl for me? Healthy and attractive, but not too beautiful."

Unkel Franz found Maria, took her home and soon they were married. Grandma adopted Jasch. As as soon as it was respectable and acceptable, Maria had a son. They named him Luke.

One day Maria got a letter. It was from Klaus:

> My *dearest Maria*,
>
> *I have found you at last. Is it too late? I am told you are married. I hope he is a loving husband to you. If he is not and you need me, please let me know and I will come.*
> "*I love you always,*
>
> Klaus

And Maria wept, knowing what her answer must be.

Part
three

1930

One year after the Wall Street crash, more than 1,000 American banks fail. This year 4,359 Americans are legally executed. Pluto, the ninth planet, is discovered. Premier Hanaguchi of Japan is assassinated. Amy Johnson flies the first solo by a woman—from England to Australia—in an open Gypsy Moth biplane. Gandhi makes his 100 mile Salt March to the sea. The British cabinet decides against a tunnel across the channel. The governors of Birmingham Hospital, England, ban the employment of married women doctors.

At the gates of Moscow, 12,000 Mennonite refugees plea for admission to Canada where thousands of jobless voters oppose immigration. Canadian Prime Minister Mackenzie King, who is fighting an election, shuts the doors to refugees. In Moscow, German ambassador Otto Auhagen meets with the refugees and appeals to President Hindenburg. Under the burden of reparations imposed by the Versailles Treaty, Germany is also in economic difficulty. Drawing on his family resources, Hindenburg provides temporary residence in Germany for 5,000 of the refugees. Stalin ships the remaining 7,000 to Siberian labour camps. They are never seen again. Mackenzie King and the Liberal Party lose the election.

Jakob is eight and starts his first year at the district English school.

20

The Meadowlark

THE EARLY SUMMER SUN was well above the horizon when Jakob finished breakfast. Grabbing his lunch pail, he sprinted down the lane to the village street where Eva waited impatiently for him. Having missed a year, he was in the same grade as Eva although he was a year older. But he didn't mind because no one else did.

Skipping and swinging their lunch pails, they walked down the street into the morning sun and the village centre. They passed the weathered single-storey building with two sets of double shuttered windows facing the street where Jakob had attended school the year before. Next winter it would be empty, used on occasional Sundays when a pastor from one of the bigger villages came to conduct church services. Eva skipped ahead and turned around to face Jakob, walking backwards, in step with him. The sun framed her head from behind and he squinted to see her laughing eyes.

"On which side of the school did you sit, Jakob?"

"Just like in church, the boys sat on the right side."

"Did you ever get a strapping?"

"No, but Henry Thiessen and I were punished one time when the teacher caught us talking in class. We had to sit behind the girls and Henry cried. It didn't bother me."

Eva giggled.

"If I were a boy, I would be terribly ashamed to sit behind the girls. I think I'd rather be strapped. Anyway, I'm glad you're coming to the English school with me. Aren't you?"

"I want to read and write English but I don't like walking so far. Especially in a dust storm. But it's fun when it rains."

"How old are these trees? I bet they're the biggest in the world."

They stood in the shadow of the black cottonwoods. A faint rustle in the branches hinted at the early morning breeze. Their heads tilted back, they strained to see the flutter of leaves against the prairie sky.

"Papa says they were here before he built our house. Old Mr. Neufeld planted them."

Jakob peered apprehensively up the driveway that curved around the red barn of the Martens' place. He picked up a throwing stone from the edge of the road and hefted it for size and weight. Then he changed his mind and tossed it away.

"Let's go. I don't want their gander to see me. He caught up with me last week and cut my legs with his spurs. I was bleeding. It hurt."

"Why did they come back from Mexico?"

"Bandits came to their village in the middle of the night to rob them and sometimes took their daughters but they always brought them back. I guess they borrowed them to clean up their dirty houses. If I had been there," he added, "I would have shot them. I wouldn't let them steal and break my things."

"But killing people is a sin."

"They aren't real people like you and me. They're Mexicans."

They passed a garden with scrubby crabapple, chokecherry and pin cherry trees and drifted toward the fence to look at a Case steam tractor, its smoke stack facing the street. Now quiet, last week the puffing monster had pulled rocks, houses and barns. It ran the only threshing machine in the village, operated by Jake, the village blacksmith.

"Jake can do anything, can't he?"

"Just about," said Jakob. "He can take two pieces of iron and make them stick together so they're like one piece. And he's strong. When he tells workers what to do they do it. They wouldn't dare to disobey."

"He makes coffins for dead people, doesn't he?"

"Yep. He makes them in the middle of the night when everybody's asleep."

"Will he ever get married?"

"Mama says he's too old. He's almost thirty."

"Papa is very old. I think he's forty-five."

The neighbouring unpainted, weather-worn cottage was half the size of the average village house. A curtain on the main floor had been partly drawn back by an invisible hand. The two children stopped, openly curious.

"Have you ever seen Mrs. Welk?"

"No," replied Jakob. "I don't think anybody sees her except the women who bring her chicken noodle soup. When Mama sends me with a pail of soup they never ask me in. She's always been sick, I guess. Her husband is grumpy. Never smiles. Papa says they are an unhappy family."

At the end of the village the street became a trail leading to the river, a mile away. The corner was known as "the pond." This spring the water reached almost to the level of the road. By summer it would dry up. They took the turn to the left.

A red-winged blackbird swooped across the water and settled on a willow, partly spreading its wings with the rise and fall of the slender branch until bird and willow swung in rhythm.

"Don't ducks look silly when they tip forward, sticking their tails in the air?"

Jakob skipped a stone over the water. In the still of the morning they heard the plop. Rings of wavelets rippled out ... out .... until they stirred the reeds near the edge of the road.

Now they hurried, they had another mile to go.

A distant melody broke over the field, the song of the meadowlark. A quarter-mile later they saw it perched on the barbed wire fence. Long billed, black-striped sides, a black V separating the yellow throat and breast.

"Mama calls it the morning sunshine bird," said Eva. "Of all the birds I think it has the most beautiful song."

Lifting its wings to fly, it fluttered frantically, then swung from the wire, upside down.

"Its foot is caught," gasped Jakob. "Its leg is twisted and broken. Give me that stick. Quick!"

She picked up a broken board beside the road and handed it to him. He stepped closer, measured the distance with a practised eye, and swung hard. The wings flapped feebly, hung limp. The beak dripped blood.

"Now it won't hurt any more," choked Eva.

Jakob drew back his arm and hurled the stick over the fence. He picked up his lunch pail and, without a word, strode briskly for school. Eva ran to catch up. A stray cloud drifted over the sun, throwing a shadow over the two children as they walked down the road.

After school, Eva was waiting for him.

"Let's go home the other way," she suggested.

His mood brightened. They walked around the side of the school building. He climbed over the fence and Eva stepped through between the boards.

They walked in the well-worn ruts of a country trail overgrown with quack grass into the setting sun. Their rambling, unconscious chatter was occasionally interrupted by the distant caw of a crow, the buzz of beetles and the *whr-r-r* of grasshopper wings. A blue dragonfly lit on a wildflower near the trail. Overhead a hawk circled and soared, wings motionless against a pale blue sky streaked with wisps of cotton cloud. A light breeze shook the bluebells on their frail stems and the buttercups snuggled to the ground.

Half a mile west, they left the trail, scampered through the ditch, through the barbed wire fence into the pasture a mile north of the village. Silverberry bushes, which grow where the virgin prairie sod has never been broken, were in full bloom.

"Don't they smell sweet?"

"Yes, I love them when the berries are ripe in fall."

Halfway to the village, they sat down at a straw stack to rest in the setting sun. He broke a straw and put it in his mouth at a rakish angle, as grownups do. A gopher, too young and curious to know danger, came close. They sat motionless until it was within inches of her foot. Uncertain what to do, Eva pulled back her foot. The animal ran a few yards and stood up on its hind legs, cautious but still curious.

She looked up at the late afternoon clouds.

"That one, there." She pointed. "It looks like an angel. See the wings?"

He shifted the straw in his mouth. She continued without waiting for his reply.

"Do you think God is up there looking down at us, listening to what we're saying?"

"I guess so. That's what Papa says. Sometimes it scares me that He

74

knows everything about me."

She sat up and turned. "Jakob, do you think I'm innocent?"

"I don't know. Why?"

"The preacher says that innocent children go to Heaven. Do you think I would go to Heaven if I died?"

He broke the straw in half. "I don't know. Why don't you ask your Mama? I'll ask mine."

The muted *whoo-oo-oo* of the four o'clock passenger train carried across the miles of open prairie. Listening intently, they heard the rushing sound of distant wheels clacking on steel rails.

"I'm hungry. Let's go." Jakob scrambled to his feet. The gopher scurried away.

A quarter-mile from home he saw the bobbing tail of Jeff coming to greet him. The dog bounded up to Eva, who rewarded him with a leftover sandwich.

21

A Letter

"JAKOB, TAKE THIS to the Giesbrechts."

It was a folded letter with a hand-drawn wavering black border, the width of his finger. The funeral notice had been delivered from another village by horse and buggy and would now be hand-carried from one house to another. In this way everyone received notice of the funeral within two days of anyone's death.

He didn't like to go to the Giesbrechts. He had heard their dog yelping in pain and tried not to think about it. The family screamed at each other and their cows looked hungry, even in summer when the grass was lush and plentiful.

As he approached the house his uneasy eyes searched the yard for the farm dog. He stepped on the flimsy porch, lifted the latch and, when he opened the door, the inner door to the kitchen was open. A taciturn youth in grimy coveralls took the letter to the other room. No words were spoken and Jakob turned to leave. As he unlatched the outer door, there was the dog, its one rheumy yellow eye fixed on him, upper lip raised, exposing a fang. A deep rumbling growl.

He backed into the vestibule, cornered. The dog moved a step forward on stiff legs, hair bristling. The growl rose to a snarl.

He screamed.

The inner door snapped open. The dog hesitated, its attention diverted by the youth in the doorway. "Did he bite you?"

"N-n-no, but he won't let me go home."

The youth reached into a box of firewood and grasped a heavy piece of poplar. As he raised his arm to strike, the animal spun for the exit and yelped as it collided with the door. The arm came down and Jakob heard the crack of wood on bone. The dog fled, limping and yelping.

"You're pale and trembling," said Mama.
In a shaking voice, he described what happened.
"You don't have to go there again." Papa paused. "There is much unhappiness in that house."

22

Cats, Dogs and Ohms

THE FIRST DOG JAKOB REMEMBERED had the long nose and fluffy coat of a sheep dog. They named him Collie. He had a natural urge to herd cattle and horses and he tried to be perfect. He rounded up livestock without fuss, watched for stragglers and kept them moving until they were in the barn to be harnessed or in the paddock to be milked. Each evening, at exactly six o'clock, he brought in the cows. He was a serious work dog and seemed to think that chasing balls was puppy play. Maybe because he was no longer a puppy. Big and soft and cuddly, he allowed Jakob to hug him.

One day Tante Anna came from the city to visit the family, with a tiny white poodle on her arm. It yap-yapped at Collie, who ignored it. But the poodle kept circling and yapping. At last Collie lost patience and sat on the poodle and the *yap-yap* rose to a screeching *yip-yip*.

Collie was a gentle and sensitive dog, easily offended by a harsh word. One day when Obraum lost his temper and yelled at Collie, the dog slunk away. For three days, whenever Obraum called him, Collie went into hiding. But he came when Jakob or Papa called him.

As the dog got older his joints began to stiffen. Getting up was painful and he moved slowly. A dog that cannot move quickly to dodge the kick of a horse or the horn of a cow can be injured or killed. And so he was no longer called on to help. Like most workers without a boss, the horses and cows became disorderly and hard to manage.

One day Papa brought home a new puppy. Petah called him Jeff and the name stuck. He was a joyful animal and fun to play with. Jakob forgot about Collie, whom he hadn't seen for days. When he asked where Collie was, Papa said he'd gone away.

Like a puppy that wouldn't grow up, Jeff was playful, quick to learn and anxious to please. Clever and nimble, he learned to walk on his hind legs, to roll over and jump through hoops. Jakob's favourite game was to place a delicious tidbit on Jeff's nose and order him to "stay." On the word "okay," he flipped the treat up, snapped it out of the air and crunched it with gusto. A quick pat on the head—"good boy, good boy"—and Jeff, tongue out and tail wagging, was ready for more. For Jeff, life was great fun. He thought every creature was a friend and would romp around with the horses rather than herd them. Because he was so much fun and a playful companion, Papa decided the farm needed another dog to do the work.

Again it was Petah, Jakob's younger brother, who named him Mutt. His right ear, up and alert, showed that he probably had a German Shepherd among his ancestors. His left ear, which flopped at midpoint, made him resemble a cocky village boy with his cap at a rakish angle but when he sat down he lost his dignity. His slumping haunches made him look silly.

Most dogs learn quickly to manage their four legs so the hind feet don't step on the front. Not Mutt. When he sniffed the trail of a gopher, his enthusiasm caused him to forget to angle-trot, and he tripped on his front feet and rolled over. When he recovered, he had lost the trail.

He was a slow learner. Several times when he chased a milk cow after he had been told to stop, Jakob slapped him, "No! No!" yet Mutt happily wagged his tail. Any voice, harsh or gentle, or the touch of a hand, even in anger, were signs to Mutt that someone loved him.

But one morning he surprised everyone. Overnight the horses had accidentally unlatched the field gate and would have escaped if Mutt had not been alert. All night, he stood guard at the gate and when a horse tried to escape he snarled and nipped at their noses.

"Good boy!"

The desire of both dogs to please people eventually got Mutt and Jeff into trouble with each other. Petah trained Jeff to jump over a stick, then through a hoop and through his arms. Then Jakob and Petah decided to make it a two-dog performance. Jakob steadied Mutt by the collar, Petah held a stick over him and Jeff jumped over the stick. With much practice, Mutt obeyed the command to stand still and Jeff jumped over him. To the delight of visitors, whenever the dogs were ordered to perform they growled and snarled at each other.

One day Mutt tried to mate with Jeff, who snarled, whipped around, the hair on his neck raised, his fangs snap-snapping. Big Mutt cowered in fear and flattened to the ground, then rolled over on his back, as dogs do when when they don't want to fight.

Some animals never lose the wildness from which they came. It may always be ready to awaken. When they chased a ball or car, maybe they imagined it was a rabbit or fox. Mutt loved to chase rabbits and Jakob often wondered what he would do if he caught one.

He was walking in the field with both dogs, watching them run in circles and sniff the ground. *What do they think about when they do that? Do they just go where their noses lead them?* Maybe Mutt was hoping for another rabbit.

The day before, Mutt had flushed a jackrabbit from a small bush and chased it. Just as he was near enough to grab it, the rabbit veered sharply to the left. Mutt didn't make the turn and the rabbit got away.

Now it happened again. A jackrabbit leaped in the air. Mutt quickly took up the chase. He remembered what had happened yesterday. Instead of following the rabbit, he. angled to the left, intending to cut the rabbit off when it veered. Of course, it kept going straight ahead!

Do rabbits laugh?

Trotting and sniffing his way back, Mutt came upon a second rabbit, a young one, feeding and completely unaware of him. Mutt wasn't about to let this one get away. The rabbit, munching away, never noticed the dog coming. Just when Mutt was close enough to grab the rabbit, he slid to a stop. This rabbit wasn't afraid of him. It hadn't run like a rabbit should. Of course, when the rabbit saw Mutt he bounded away in a panic. Maybe he laughed, too, when he was safely home.

One day Mutt gave everyone a surprise.

Andy was a magnificent black horse with powerful shoulders and a flying mane. This day he decided not to come in from the field.

"Mutt, sic 'im!"

Andy laid back his ears and bared his teeth. Mutt circled, growling and snapping his fangs. Andy turned around and around, his ears back, looking for a chance to lash out a kick powerful enough to kill Mutt.

A hoof flashed. Mutt didn't move or duck to avoid the blow, but the blow missed him. Before the hoof was down, Mutt nipped Andy's heel. They circled again. This time Jakob was directly behind them when Andy kicked. He saw how Mutt escaped injury. A horse kicks slightly outward, never straight back. By staying exactly in the centre, Mutt found a safe place where no kick could strike him.

"Papa, is a dog as smart as people?"

Papa didn't say anything and Jakob thought maybe he hadn't heard. But he was thinking.

"Smarter, in some ways. People are smart in a different way. A farmer knows what each cow, pig and chicken needs. I know what our neighbour needs and what you need. But, clever as they are, Mutt and Jeff know only what they need. They would never think about providing food for you or me or any creature that cannot feed itself."

"Are people like that? Do some of them know only what they need?"

He was thinking again. "I'm afraid not even that."

Most villagers banned dogs and cats from their homes. Houses, they said, are for people and barns for animals. Mama and Papa would have agreed with their neighbours but only partly. When Mutt wasn't bringing the cows into the paddock for milking or herding the horses into the barn to be harnessed, he lay on the porch with a wary eye and ear for intruders.

In winter, everyone, both people and animal, tracked snow into the house. To absorb the water that melted from the snow, sawdust was spread over the floor of the kitchen. Several times a week it was swept up, burned in the kitchen range and replaced with fresh sawdust.

Papa played a game with Jeff. Taking him by the scruff of the neck and tail, he swung Jeff back and forward, releasing him to slide along the floor. Jeff tried frantically to stop but the sawdust gave him no footing. When he eventually slid to a stop, he turned around, growling and snapping at Papa, who raised his arms so that Jeff could not reach them. Papa thought it great fun until Jeff realized that the legs belonged to Papa too, and bit him, gently, in the calf.

"Clever Jeff," Papa laughed.

On winter nights, Jeff found the highest snowdrift from which he could observe the farmyard. Before lying down, he turned a few circles, coiled his body and flipped his tail over his nose to shield it from the wind. But in daylight hours and evenings when the family was up and about, he dozed under the kitchen table where his paws were safe from careless human feet. On occasion, when he awoke and stretched to change position, a silent waft might escape. If Mama's delicate nose whiffed his lapse she quickly put him out in the cold.

One bitter winter day, as Jeff dozed under the table, Mama paused with the knife in the middle of a cucumber and sniffed.

"Jeff, did you ... ?" As she briskly strode across the kitchen to the broom hanging on the wall, the dog dashed for the door.

"Shame on you. Out, out!"

As he scrambled out, she gave him a rap with the whisk end which deeply offended him, not knowing what he had done to deserve it.

She was slicing the second cucumber when Papa, reading the *Post*, chuckled. Softly, he chuckled. Suspicious, she looked at him.

"Did you ... ?"

His eyes twinkled. And he chuckled.

"*You* did it! Poor Jeff. I blamed him. I should put *you* out in the snow!"

She opened the door. "Come in, Jeff. Come in." The dog crawled in, cowering, half wagging his tail, not sure what to expect.

"Here, Jeff. Good dog." Mama poured something in his dish.

"Is that *Summaborscht?*" asked Papa. "Wasn't that our dinner?"

"It was. Today it will be peanut butter and *Supsil* and bread."

On summer nights, Benny the tomcat divided his time between prowling the farm for mice and snarling at other cats. On cold winter nights he slept in the barn but, when daylight came, he joined the household. He enjoyed long conversations with Mama. If no lap was offered, he slept on the warm floor under the kitchen range or sat in the window to watch the snowbirds in the maple grove.

At *Faspa*, Papa sat in his oak chair at the head of the oilcloth-covered kitchen table, Mama at his right, the coffee kettle on the corner between them. Jakob sat on Papa's left, on a bench along the wall, his back to the window. Benny sat on the window sill behind him. When the cat reached out to tap him on the shoulder, Jakob gave him a crumb or tasty tidbit from his plate.

Jakob was always glad when visitors came to *Faspa* because that's when Mama would put out three kinds of *Supsil*: pin cherry, gooseberry and chokecherry. He liked the tart gooseberry, especially on bread hot out of the brick oven that Papa had built under the maple trees.

One day, an *Ohm* of the church came to visit Papa, perhaps to talk about a family that needed help or a member of the flock whose wife had curled her hair or indulged in other vanities. Papa couldn't hear very well. So the two elders could converse more easily, Jakob gave his window seat to the *Ohm*. As Papa listened intently to the point the *Ohm* was making, Mama's eyes scanned the table, anxious she might have forgotten something.

Jakob, who sat across the table from the guest, saw Benny, unnoticed, jump on the window sill behind the *Ohm* as Mama poured coffee. Carefully tilting his coffee cup, the guest poured some in his saucer to cool. As he raised the saucer to his lips to blow, Benny tapped him on the shoulder.

With a yelp and a hearty fart, the *Ohm* leaped to his feet, slopping coffee all over the table. With one jump, Benny cleared the table and scrambled under the kitchen stove.

"We never keep cats in our house!" growled the livid and shaking *Ohm*, face flushed.

Mama quickly rose from her chair, wiped up the mess and refilled his cup. Jakob looked up to catch her eye to see what she was thinking, but she stared hard at the coffee kettle. With the corner of her apron she wiped her eyes. There might have been a twinkle in Papa's eyes, but Jakob thought he must have been mistaken because Papa's expression was as sober as the bishop's.

Mama said to put Benny out of the house, but the cat was too frightened to come out. The *Ohm* forgot why he came and seemed in a hurry. He quickly finished his coffee, turned his cup upside down in the saucer and left.

He never came for *Faspa* again.

23

De Ensen

THE OTHER MEN IN THE VILLAGE took no notice of little boys, but Mr. Ens always said *Gondach* to Jakob when they met on the street and sometimes even took the pipe out of his mouth to talk about the weather. But when Jakob was with Papa, the two men exchanged only a one-word greeting. Without a smile.

"*Gondach.*"

"*Gondach.*"

Jakob had seen the inside of all the other homes when he delivered invitations to funerals, auction sales or marriage betrothals. But he'd never seen the Ensen and they were never invited anywhere. It was a big house and the paint was flaking off. Papa said you could always tell a well-built house if the roof and shutters were straight. Everything was straight, but the house looked like a white cat that doesn't wash itself anymore.

Papa and Mama never talked about the Ensen. Just like they weren't there. But the house was there, its windows staring at Jakob when he walked by. He saw Mrs. Ens only when she worked in her garden. He didn't know what she looked like, close up. People talked about a boy from the city who sometimes came to visit them, but no one had ever talked to him and no one seemed to know anything about him.

"Mama, why do you never invite the Ensen for pig killing? He always talks nice to me when I see him on the street."

"I need more wood for the stove. Will you fill up the box?"

After a while, he stopped asking questions.

Many years later he asked Knals about the Ensen.

"You didn't know?" The older boys must have talked about it and thought everyone else knew. "I guess you were too young to understand."

Mr. Ens came to Canada from Iowa, married a sister of the family that founded the village, bought a farm nearby and built a house big enough for a large family. Everyone could see they had more money than most Rosenheimers because they hired Suschje, a teenage girl, to milk the cows and help in the garden, and a young man to do the farm work.

Three years later, the Ensen had no children.

"The Peters have been married four years and have three children already. And the Wiebes, married for ten years, have eight," said Mr. Ens. "What is it with us? It's three years now and you have still not given me a son, or even a daughter."

"How do you know it's my fault?"asked Mrs. Ens.

"What are we going to do? There is no life for us without children. That is why I bought this farm, built this house and you planted a garden. People give their lives for the future of their children. We have none. Who will take care of us when we are old?"

She thought about it for a moment, then exclaimed. "Why didn't I think of it before? If only I had a handmaiden."

"What do you mean? You want another *Kjäkshe*? You have Suschje and that's more than anyone else has in Rosenheim. Why don't you call her a handmaiden and be done with it, if that's what you want."

"It's in the Bible! If it was right for God's chosen people it must be right for us."

"What are you talking about?"

She opened her Bible.

"Here it is, Genesis 30. Jakob and Rachel couldn't have children either and it says here '*She gave him her handmaid to wife and Jakob went in unto her and she conceived and bore Jakob a son.*' Maybe Suschje could give us a child. Maybe many children. And she would be a member of our family instead of just a *Kjäkshe*. The children could call her *Tante*." Her face broke into a smile. "It would be so nice to have a large family."

"But would she do it?"

"She is obedient and will do what you tell her. We will promise to adopt the child, if there is one."

It was a boy and the Ensen were very, very happy. But troubles were yet to come. The *Ohms* of the church called Mr. Ens to *Donnadach* meeting and sentenced the Ensen to be shunned for two weeks. They were to be treated as if they did not exist, not to be listened or spoken to.

But the villagers had daughters and their daughters had daughters. And the two weeks never ended.

When the boy turned fifteen, he ran away. He returned to visit the Ensen only when he needed money.

fences and Neighbours

"IF YOU HAD LIFE to live over again, would you do anything different?"

"Nothing."

Papa was visiting a former neighbour who was dying.

The farm village was settled at the turn of the century when land was cheap, surveying was imprecise and the placement of markers was casual. Papa bought the property next to the neighbour, erected half a mile of barbed wire fence, built a barn, a house and storage buildings. Decades later the neighbour declared the fence that Papa built was six inches inside his property and demanded he uproot it and move it over.

The time and labour to tear down and rebuild half a mile of fence would have been more than the value of the farmland lost or gained by either neighbour. Papa offered to pay for the disputed land at going prices. The neighbour sued. The justice of the peace ruled that since Papa had erected the fence in good faith, the neighbour should build a second fence where he believed the boundary to be. This created a no man's land between the two fences, half a mile long by six inches wide which received a short column in the city paper and much community attention.

From that day on the neighbour harassed Papa at every opportunity. Persuaded that he should live in peace so far as it was within his power to do so, Papa showed great restraint. But eventually the neighbour pressed him beyond endurance. It came about in this way.

When Papa built the house in 1906, he had planted maples on the west side. A pipe from the kitchen drain supplied them with waste water. After twenty-five years the trees were tall enough to shade the wall and part of the roof. On hot summer afternoons when the sun dipped behind the trees, a cool breeze drifted through the open window and across the table where the family gathered to replenish their energies over *Faspa*, with a cup of *Prips* and fruit *Supsil* spread on fresh home-baked *Zwieback*.

One summer day, the neighbour and his sons were seen to pace off an area of his property windward of the beloved maple grove. Next day a row of fenceposts was sunk and wire fencing unrolled. By day's end, the sty was occupied by a small herd of pigs. A week later the foul stench of hog dung polluted the air and Mama closed the window. No longer could the Schellenbergs look forward to *Faspa* on a hot day in the cool of a breeze from the shadow of the maples. The health department, friends and relatives urged Papa to lodge a complaint. Being a man of peace, he declined.

As winter approached, the neighbour assembled materials to construct a shelter for his animals. Hog barns in the village settlement were of simple and inexpensive construction. A frame of poplar logs or old lumber was covered with wheat straw in which the pigs would happily burrow to keep warm in winter and cool in summer.

Instead of hauling the straw from a stack and forking it over the frame, the neighbour set up a threshing machine windward of the pig sty. The thresher blew the straw and fine chaff over the frame and beyond, drifting over fence, garden, farmyard and into the summer kitchen.

Papa was working in the shop when his two oldest sons walked to the rack where the long-handled tools were kept. Knals picked up an axe and Obraum hefted a sledge hammer. Papa asked what they had in mind.

"We're going to fix the neighbour's threshing machine."

"That will not be necessary. Knals, hitch the gelding to the buggy. Obraum and I will visit the justice of the peace. Don't do anything rash while we are gone. Wait for us."

The spirited gelding took at least three hours to make the return trip and, before Papa returned, a car drove on the neighbour's yard and a Mountie stepped out. A few minutes later the steady roar of the threshing machine wound down and died out. The operator disassembled the equipment and towed it away. When Papa came home, the Mountie came over, looked at the straw-covered yard, the buildings and the garden and drove away.

The justice of the peace fined the neighbour five dollars and awarded Papa sixteen dollars in damages. For the following twenty years they lived side by side in harmony, if not in friendship.

"Is there anything that troubles you about our many years as neighbours?" asked Papa.

"Yes," he replied. "There is one thing."

"Is it a burden that I can lift from your mind?"

"It's the twenty-one dollars I had to pay."

"Would you feel better if I paid you back?"

"Yes."

Papa pulled out his wallet and placed two tens and a one on the table beside the bed. Two weeks later they buried the neighbour.

"I hope he is now at peace," said Papa.

25

Sheep

"MAYBE WE CAN FIND another way for animals to help us run the farm," said Papa. At *Faspa*, when the sun was halfway between its highest point and the horizon, he spoke of doing something new and different. He got pleasure from arousing curiosity and held it as long as he could, with long pauses, revealing his plans a bit at a time. Mama fell into the trap first.

"What do you mean, help? We have a dog to round up the cows and cats to catch mice. What can a cow do except give us milk?"

"I'm thinking of the weeds that grow between the boards of the lumber pile or around the trees and between the wheels of farm machinery on the yard. We can't get at the stuff with a scythe or hoe."

A few weeks later, three ewes and one ram chomped weeds and grass under plows, at the edge of fences and buildings and where no one had seen it. And when they lay in the shade of a wagon, eyes half closed, leisurely munching, they looked happy and satisfied.

As summer came to an end, the days grew shorter and the wool on the sheep grew longer and thicker.

"I can make some nice quilts," said Mama.

In early spring, before all the snow was gone, the ewes gave birth to five lambs. When they weren't sucking their mothers' milk they were bouncing, jumping and hopping. The tin roof of the hen house, where their little hoofs made a clatter when they danced, was their favourite place.

"I'm glad we don't live in it any more," laughed Papa. " It was the first house I built when we moved on the homestead."

"You lived in one room?"

"I think we were just as happy as we are in the two rooms we have now," said Papa. "Of course, now we are six. Then, it was only your mother and I and our first baby. We were happy." He turned to the blacksmith shop. "Help me sharpen the shears. You can crank the wheel. Tomorrow we shear the sheep."

Knals and Obraum held the sheep and turned it on its back, stomach, side and every other way for Papa to snip away the wool. The lambs were bewildered and cried *ba-a-a-a,* and their mothers, not knowing why their little ones were upset and unable to see them, cried *baw-aw-aw.*

After the sheep were sheared, the wool was rolled up and tied in bundles for washing. To kill the ticks that lived in the wool and fed on animal blood, the sheep were sprayed with sheep dip and set free.

When the lambs saw this naked monster—whom they didn't know—come at them, they panicked and ran, crying for their mothers. And their mothers, who understood their cry of fear but didn't know the reason, ran after their lambs with a loud *baw-aw-aw.* The lambs tried to escape, bounced over their mothers and cried out in alarm. Their mothers, not knowing that the lambs didn't recognize them, were bewildered.

By late afternoon, they had discovered each other; the ewes were nursing their lambs and everyone was happy.

26

Anna, Isaac and Archie

ANNA WAS A JOYFUL AND GIFTED CHILD, making up tunes on the piano by the age of three. Her sunny disposition, blond curls and blue eyes attracted attention wherever she went. When the renegades had struck their village in Russia, her family was visiting distant relatives and was thus saved the savagery that fell upon their neighbours.

In Russia, Anna's father had been a machinist, her mother a nurse in the community hospital. In Canada, unemployed tradesmen were driving taxicabs and nurses were scrubbing floors. Immigrants were admitted to the country only on the condition they work in agriculture. Anna's father became a field hand and her mother learned to milk cows.

The girl had always been a clever and industrious student, willful and independent, the beneficiary of refinement and indulgence. It was painful for her parents, who'd had servants in Russia, to see their daughter work as a domestic in the city.

"We don't want to worry about your safety and have arranged for you to stay at a Mädchenheim."

The 'maiden-home' was created to protect vulnerable young Mennonite women from abuse and exploitation by employers. Half a dozen young women shared a rented house with a matron who looked after her charges, occasionally with more zeal than was appreciated.

A graceful and outgoing young woman with a gift for language, Anna quickly found work in a medical clinic. When the doctor's wife offered an elegantly furnished spare bedroom in the family home with free use of library and piano, she packed her few personal possessions in a bag and moved in. Within a week the doctor's wife was rushed to the hospital for an emergency appendectomy and a month later Anna found herself pregnant. It was unthinkable for the new immigrants to confront an *Englaenda* doctor, a member of a respected profession. Why would anyone believe them?

And so Anna's older brother was appointed to find a husband for her.

"My sister Anna asked about you. Why don't you call on her?"

The question bewildered Isaac, who had long ago accepted the reality of his status. His family was of the landless, living on the generosity of a land owner who allowed them to build a modest two-room house on a corner of his farm.

Anna had rejected countless desirable marriage prospects. Why would a beautiful girl from an educated *Russlaenda* family who had a job in the city be interested in an Old Colony labourer? Maybe the fellows had put her up to teasing him. They liked to see him lose his temper. However, she overcame his suspicions and convinced Isaac that she wanted him.

Two weeks later, on a Saturday afternoon, their betrothal was celebrated and banns were announced at the Sunday church services. Isaac looked forward with impatience to visit his relatives in the week that followed, with Anna on his arm. He would show them! To his disappointment Anna pleaded illness.

On the evening of their wedding they retired to the attic bedroom of Anna's parents. All was quiet for a few minutes.

A scream of terror.

"No, no, Isaac. No!"

Anna's brother sprang up the stairs. He caught Isaac's arm as he was about to tip the kerosene lamp over the bed. In the violent struggle of rage, fear and panic, her brother finally subdued Isaac who fled from the house.

The following day, after Isaac's family convinced him it would be more discrete and less shameful if he took up his husbandly duties as if nothing had happened, he left for the city to look for work.

"Why did you tell him?" her father asked.

"When I was a little girl you made me promise never to tell a lie."

Isaac found work as a construction labourer in the city and built a house with two bedrooms. One for him and one for Anna. For fifty years neither entered the bedroom of the other except when Anna swept the floor and made the bed. They spoke only of the day's activities and, except when they had visitors, ate separately, first Isaac, then Anna.

The boy was named Archie.

A real *Bengel*, Archie painted dirty words and pictures on the neighbours' garbage cans and threw stones at passing cars. When he finished high school he got a job as a casual worker, saved his money and bought a secondhand Ford Model A roadster. He never took out girls as Isaac hoped he would. When the war came he joined the air force. Isaac was proud of "my son Archie" in his uniform, especially the wings on his chest. On embarkation leave, Archie grasped his tearful father's hand and hugged his mother who had long ago forgotten how to cry.

"Don't worry about me. I'll be back for my roadster. Take care of it for me."

Isaac raised the car on blocks to take the weight off the tires. He polished the paint until it gleamed. And he rubbed the leather upholstery with dressing. Then he covered it with a new canvas tarpaulin for Archie's return.

Two weeks after Isaac got the telegram that Archie was missing from a bombing raid, Jakob received a blue aerogramme in the mail, stamped by the censor and addressed to him in Archie's writing.

Dear cousin Jakob,

I was on my first mission yesterday. Pretty wild. Tomorrow I celebrate my twenty-first—maybe another mission. Whatever you do, don't do what I did. It's not what you think it is.

Your bastard cousin,
Archie

A letter from the other world, from *there*. Now he was gone. They would never talk about it.

At first, a numb feeling. Then grief. And anger. He wanted to follow Archie. To strike back at what had become a personal enemy.

Don't do what I did. It's not what you think it is.

Isaac cursed God, the Germans and his government for taking

Archie. He swore and he wept and he prayed. Anna said nothing. He sold the roadster and the house. They moved West. He returned to the Old Colony church of his father which he had long ago abandoned.

Anna sat, alone, in silence, as she had for so long.

Isaac fell ill and was taken to a Mennonite *Altenheim* where Anna visited him every day. She arranged his pillows, combed his wisp of hair, sat in silence while he dozed. She arranged a funeral in the Old Colony church which she had never attended.

Isaac left everything, including the house, to the church, but the bishop told Anna the church would not accept her home.

She sold the house and furnishings and made a big bonfire in the backyard. She met with a lawyer in the city who wouldn't tell anyone where she went but said she was all right. She left no forwarding address. It was rumoured she bought a big old house in the city where she welcomed young girls who were in trouble.

No one ever heard from her again.

27

Exploration and Discovery

JAKOB MUST HAVE BEEN VERY YOUNG, before he could think or remember, when he was first told not to touch it. He knew he shouldn't but didn't know why. There were other things he'd been told not to touch or do, but they made sense. You could get hurt by touching a hot stove or standing behind a horse. But touching it didn't hurt, not even a little bit.

He did a lot of thinking but was careful about talking. Sometimes talking created problems. Especially questions. The wrong questions reminded Mama of things for him to do.

"Fill the woodbox."

"Round up the cows."

"Weed the garden."

How was a fellow to know what he shouldn't ask when there was so much he didn't know? How could Maria, at the other end of the village, have a baby when she wasn't married? He thought more about it later when he was weeding carrots in the hot summer sun.

Another thing puzzled him: hugging. He'd seen people hug, mostly women. Especially Aunt Agnes and Aunt Lisa. Sometimes Jeff, the dog, would hug him in a funny way. It felt good when Jeff wrapped his forelegs around his leg. But Mama would smack Jeff and speak harshly. And when he asked why, it turned out to be a wrong question. He wasn't sure if it was bad to hug people (no one hugged him) or if it was bad to feel good. And he didn't know whom to ask. The boys in the village would make fun of questions that he didn't think were funny at all.

One summer day he was in the kitchen turning the butter churn. From time to time he stopped to look at the little window in the lid. If it was white he kept churning until it was clear. When it was clear and he heard the slosh of buttermilk followed by the thump of butter, it was done.

Papa sat, legs crossed, elbow on the family table, reading his favourite Mennonite weekly, the *Steinbach Post*. Mama was frying smoked *Wurst* for dinner, the corner of her apron wrapped around her hand to grasp the hot pan. From where she stood she could see the entrance to the farmyard through the kitchen window.

"The *Hingst* is here!" she exclaimed.

Her voice carried the anxiety she always felt when important or strange visitors came on the yard. If the bishop or the Raleigh salesman entered the house she was never quite certain what was expected of her. She was anxious to do what was right and proper for important people. Although she loved company, the family usually ate alone because she was afraid the homemade bread and preserves would not be good enough for people who could afford store-bought food. She liked people and they liked her. She could carry on a conversation with almost anyone when Papa was out of the house. Even in English.

Papa gave no indication of hearing. His eyes shifted to the top of the page. Jakob was never sure what was going on in Papa's mind but suspected that he quietly enjoyed her anxiety, although he would have denied it. His sincerity appeared genuine and he would have been offended if it had been questioned.

"Can't you hear? The *Hingst* is here. Hurry!"

Slowly, Papa uncrossed his legs, clunking his boot on the wooden floor. Deliberately, he folded the newspaper and stood up, twisting his hip to ease the bind in the crotch of his overalls, and ambled to the door. Mama impatiently glanced from the window to Papa and back again. After assuring herself that the visitor made no effort to come to the door and that Papa was safely outdoors, she sighed and turned her attention to the sausages.

"Is the *Hingst* staying for dinner?"

She started and looked at Jakob. Her lips tightened but the corners of her eyes looked crinkly. She dabbed an eye with her apron.

"His name is Martens. The *Hingst* is his horse. Yes, he's staying for dinner. And don't ask any more questions."

"Can I look? The butter is done."

"Yes, but stay inside."

Through the window he saw Papa lean against a bright red two-wheeled cart, his foot on the hub of the wheel. His head was tilted, the unconscious habit of the hard of hearing. Ohmke Martens seemed uncertain of speech, his eyes avoiding Papa's as he explained something that seemed to interest his listener.

It was the grandest horse. His black coat rippled as the Percheron arched his powerful neck. The thick mane was cropped, the tail braided and tied with a red ribbon. White fetlocks fell over four restless hooves. The nickel-studded harness gleamed in the sun.

The great horse whinnied and pawed the ground. An answering whinny came from the barn. He strained at the bit and tossed his head. The driver tightened his hold on the reins and spoke to the horse which seemed to settle him down.

The horse had the biggest thing Jakob ever saw—and it was growing longer. Wouldn't it be something to have one like that ....

"Jakob, go up in the attic and get the butter bowl. It's on a box near the mangle."

He reluctantly turned from the window as Papa walked to the barn and the visitor stepped down to unhook the traces.

Jakob found the large wooden bowl in its place at the far end of the attic. As he turned to walk down the stairs he glanced out the gable window and saw Papa lead Nell, the little brown mare, out of the barn. The driver, leading the black *Hingst*, followed them around and behind the barn, out of sight.

"Jakob! I'm waiting for the bowl."

After dinner the driver and Papa hitched the big horse to the cart and Jakob watched him drive away, the driver's head bobbing with each long stride of the *Hingst*. Papa walked to the barn and Jakob skipped back to the house.

He enjoyed fresh buttermilk, with bits of golden butter floating on top. Seated on the bench at the oilcloth-covered family table, he watched Mama squeeze the moisture out of the bright yellow butter. As she tightened her strong bony hand, the butter oozed out between her fingers. When a spoonful of cloudy water accumulated, she poured it into a bowl. Jakob swallowed the last of the buttermilk and wiped his mouth on his shirt sleeve.

"Why doesn't he trot his horse? I wanted to see him go real fast. Even Nell, pulling a four-wheeled buggy, can go faster."

"I guess he doesn't want his horse to get tired. It's a very valuable horse."

"Why is a *Hingst* more valuable than Nell?"

"Why don't you go and play with Henry?"

Beside the porch he picked up a T-shaped stick and a heavy steel ring salvaged from a wheelbarrow. He gave the ring a rolling start with his right hand. With his left, he grasped the long end of the stick and, with the crossbar, deftly pushed the rolling ring ahead, up the lane and down the village street to Henry's place.

Through the board fence he saw Henry under a crabapple tree, aligning his miniature steam tractor and threshing machine. Although it looked like a J. I. Case steam tractor in every detail, including the spinning governor, it was driven by an old alarm clock mechanism. And the threshing machine was driven by a hand-cranked pulley. It had been made mostly of wood by his older brother, Jake, who operated the original from which it had been copied. Henry was envied by every boy in the village. But he was selective about his playmates. Like Jakob, he took care of things.

"You put sand in the feeder and I'll turn the crank."

"I don't want to play, Henry. Let's talk."

"About what?" He moved the water wagon to the rear of the steam tractor and connected the hose.

"What's a *Hingst?*"

Henry looked up and thought about the question, frowning as he prepared to reply. Jakob asked Henry about a lot of things. Henry was older but not too old to remember what it was like to be two years younger.

"A *Hingst* is a Papa horse. Like the one that was here today. You know how horses do it?"

And then he told Jakob about *Hingsts* and mares, bulls and cows, and that roosters were for other things besides eating. When Jakob asked him a question for which Henry didn't have a ready answer—and there were many of them—he hesitated for only a moment. Jakob was younger and expected him to know. Henry hardly ever disappointed him.

"That's how you were born, too," he said.

"You mean ... Papa did that to Mama? She would never let him do a thing like that!"

At *Faspa*, that afternoon, he didn't feel hungry. He liked to talk at the table. Too much, Papa said. Today he couldn't think of anything. And his stomach didn't feel good.

"You feel sick today?" asked Mama.

"No," he said, avoiding her eyes.

"Then eat," said Papa.

He ate, ran outside and vomited. He sat on the steps, Jeff's head on his lap.

"How're you feeling?" Papa, behind him. Sometimes voices tell more than words.

"Better."

"It's always better after vomiting." Papa walked to the blacksmith shop, head down, in his steady and deliberate stride.

After that, Jakob was often with the older village boys. At first he was taken aback when they used words that were wrong at home. Words they learned from their big brothers who visited other villages. They called one another names and they laughed. But when Jakob tried it the words didn't sound funny and he was embarrassed when nobody laughed. And so he mostly listened. After a while nobody laughed. Dirty talk wasn't fun any more.

One rainy overcast Sunday when they were in a neighbour's barn, the conversation turned to a riddle they had never solved.

"What happens when a fellow does it with a cow or a sheep?"

"My uncle told me you get a half-animal, half-man. He has a book with a picture about Greece where they believed in other gods. It shows the body of a bull with four legs and the arms of a man with a spear in his hand. It must be true, because books don't lie."

"That must be how the devil was born. He looks like a man but his feet are like a goat's and he has horns on his head. And a tail, too."

"What do they do with all those who are born that way? Why don't we ever see anyone like that?"

"Maybe they kill them."

"Oh, no. You can't kill people. Even half-people. That would be a sin."

"My brother says they put them in an asylum and lock them up so no one ever sees them. He saw the place. It has a big stone wall and men with rifles at each corner."

"If you do it to yourself you go insane and they put you in there, too."

"Let's play catch." Then someone remembered it was raining.

Years later, one of the boys said he tried it one winter night by lantern light, when he went to do the evening chores. The cow stepped back and knocked him off the stool.

In Jakob's home there was only one woman, Mama. His only sister Katrina had died when she was less than a year old, before he was born. It would be fun to have a girl around. Maybe he could see how she looked without clothes. He looked forward to the arrival of Helen.

Papa said the government would pay fifteen dollars a month, to be divided equally between the worker and the boss. Some farmers took all the money for themselves. A very few gave it all to the girl.

At first Jakob was shy. He didn't know how to talk to her, but Helen soon put him at ease. She teased him, which he enjoyed. Jakob liked to hear her laugh. He talked to her about the many things on his mind and she always listened. She never made him feel foolish like the boys in the village did. Once she said that Jakob was smart for a boy of his age. Working with her wasn't like work. It was always fun.

One day when they were stacking fresh-mown hay behind the barn, she tripped him with her foot.

"I bet you can't throw me down," she laughed.

Jakob dropped his pitchfork and, taking her by the shoulders, pushed her backwards. Surprised at how easy it was, he lost his balance and fell on her. Laughing, he pinned her down firmly.

"Don't be so rough." She stopped laughing. But she wasn't angry. And then he felt her softness and a strange but nice feeling somewhere inside himself.

"What are you doing?"

It was Papa, who had come around the barn, unnoticed.

Helen blushed, shook him off and ran to the house.

Jakob tried to explain to Papa but the words didn't sound right. When your feelings are mixed up, what you say doesn't sound like what you mean and it only gets worse when you talk. And when you stop talking the quiet doesn't sound right either.

At supper, nobody talked much and Helen looked only at her plate. She finished before anyone else and left the table. When Jakob followed and asked her what was the matter she didn't answer. And when he teased her she didn't smile like she always did. He felt unhappy because he didn't want her to be angry with him. Maybe he'd gotten her into trouble with Mama or Papa.

Next morning Papa hitched Nell to the buggy. Helen put her cardboard box of clothes behind the seat and climbed up beside Mama. Mama said she was taking Helen home to her village. Nobody explained and Jakob didn't ask questions. But he was sure it had something to do with boys and girls wrestling and that girls were soft and felt good but maybe it was something that couldn't be talked about. Maybe it had something to do with the way people had babies but that's not what Helen and he were doing. He didn't feel wrong, but it was confusing.

And so he stayed home to pick the beetles off the potato plants and weed and hoe the rows of vegetables. All summer Jakob did a lot of thinking. That year they had the cleanest garden in the village with the sweetest watermelons, the biggest cabbages and the plumpest tomatoes.

28

The Seasons

WHEREVER THEY ROAMED, for centuries Mennonite villagers and their ancestors adapted their traditions and knowledge of nature to preserve and store perishable foods. In late fall, when the frost came to stay and the days grew short, they gathered on each other's farms and homes to continue what generations of ancestors had done.

To feed the family, four hogs of four hundred pounds each provided the lard, head cheese, sausage, ham, bacon, liverwurst and spare ribs for a family of six ... a pound and a half of pig for a pound of Schellenberg.

"Jakob, get up. *Schwien schlachten!*"

He wanted to stay in his warm bed. His schoolmates would sleep for two more hours.

As he shivered to the outhouse, the shadows of couples trudged up the lane and through the fresh snow to the house where the helpers shared an early breakfast before the work ahead. In front of the barn, steam rose from two giant cast iron cookers.

In the outdoor pig enclosure, a pig and Papa faced each other. He knelt on one leg, aimed the Belgian-made bolt action .22. The pig lowered its head, motionless, as if hypnotized.

Crack!

The pig sagged, its front legs buckling. A man with a knife ran forward.

It was rolled onto a sled, blood trailing on the white snow to the barn where it was lifted on a ladder to a scalding trough. Boiling water was dipped from the cooker and poured on the carcass, which was scraped until it glowed a shiny pink.

Hoisted upside down with rope and pulley to a beam in the barn, the carcass was ready for the "out-taker." Jake, who operated the steam-powered threshing machine, built coffins and repaired broken equipment, knew the inner mysteries of hogs. He flourished knife and axe until the carcass hung in two pieces. Two husky men hoisted them, one at a time, onto tables where men were poised with newly sharpened knives.

Other men carried pails of intestines to the summer kitchen where women emptied them, turning them inside out and scraping the linings with kitchen knives on wooden boards. After washings and rinsing under boiling water, the intestines were returned to the barn where the meat had been ground, peppered and salted to the sausage maker's taste. The clean intestines were slipped over the tube, the machine cranked and meat oozed into the intestine, now a casing for a sausage.

To check the accuracy of his aim, Papa split and examined the skull to refresh his memory of its structure and the direction of the bullet to the brain.

When the light of day had turned to amber, the hams were salted, the bacon rolled and tied, the tables scrubbed. After a supper of spare ribs and liverwurst shared by the light of kerosene lamps and lanterns, the guests donned their winter coats and boots and mitts to go home. A young married couple, who would butcher their own hog next year, stayed for Mama's gift of sausage and ribs and a small pail of lard.

"When you and Papa help to butcher other people's pigs, why does he always take the rifle? Don't others kill their own?"

"The first year we lived in the village and were invited to help the neighbours, Papa was very upset the way they did it. They just threw the pig down and cut its throat. And so he offered to shoot the next pig. And the next."

It was January and everything was frozen, even the bins of wheat in the granary.

"Now we'll cover the frozen meat with wheat. When the spring thaw comes, the meat will stay frozen for at least another month." Papa knew how everything worked. In some ways, he seemed smarter than Jake but, in other ways, Jake knew more.

When most of the snow had melted, Papa said it was time to smoke the meat for summer.

"We'll need a load of straw from the field."

Obraum and Jakob took the hayrack off the bobsled and tipped it back on a four-wheeled wagon to which a team of horses had been hitched. While they were gone, Papa and Knals lifted a feed cooker out of its jacket and connected it to a smoke-box with stovepipes. Sausages, bacon and hams were hung from the iron bars that crossed the top of the box.

Later in the afternoon, Obraum and Jakob returned with a load of straw and dumped a small pile near the smoker assembly.

"Not too much, not too close." Papa was always on the alert for any accident, any possibility of a fire spreading out of control. Jakob was assigned to feed and watch the fire.

The cooker jacket, without the pot, was like a round barrel of about thirty inches in diameter and height. The fire could be stoked with straw through a small door in the side and it had a cover to keep down the flames and let the smoke flow out the stovepipe to the smoker, which contained the ham and other meats to be cured.

For the rest of the afternoon and into the evening, Jakob kept stoking the fire, almost smothering it to produce the heaviest smoke. Overnight, the meat cooled and in the morning it was hung from rafters in the cellar.

Through the summer they had smoked ham and sausage and bacon to make a variety of traditional Mennonite soups and meat dishes, including *borscht*, cabbage and pea soup.

In fall, when the frost came to stay, another four pigs were fat and ready to restart the cycle.

29

Unkel Hein

It was a summer day and Mama was singing *"Gott ist die Liebe"* as she rolled dough in little balls for the wedding of Unkel Hein, her youngest brother.

"He is twenty-seven already. I thought he would never get a wife. And he is such a good person, he was always kind to me."

"This girl he is marrying," Papa looked up from the newspaper, "She is very *stolt*. She wears earrings and lipstick and cuts her hair. Is that good?"

Mama smiled. "She is such a happy person. I like to be with her."

"Yes, she laughs a lot. Maybe too much." Papa folded the paper and reached for his straw hat. "Time to feed the pigs." He picked up the slop pails and after he closed the door behind him Mama said, more to herself than to Jakob, who watched her expert hands manipulate the dough, "I hope he doesn't say anything about her jewelry and make-up. I feel badly when he offends people."

"Why does he do that?"

"Jakob, our church says it's vanity, and vanity is bad."

"Do you think it's bad, Mama?"

She shook her head. "I don't know, Jakob. I don't know."

"And is this my new nephew?"

"Yes, this is Jakob."

"Now you must have a piece of my wedding cake, Jakob. But first, let me hug you."

He'd never been hugged like that. She was beautiful, dressed in white like an angel and she smelled like the flowers in Mama's garden.

The cake was the best he ever tasted.

He watched her talk to grownups. She smiled and laughed and everyone laughed with her. Unkel Hein always had his arm around her. Papa never did that to Mama.

"Where did she go?"

"She is getting dressed. They have a long way to drive to their homestead at Sonningdale, where they will live."

She was wearing a bright red dress and when she hugged him, he inhaled a scent that was different from the first. He looked down the front of her dress and wanted to rest his head. And then they said goodbye.

The Model T coupe had boxes stacked on the roof and rolls of bedding and clothes overflowing the rumble seat.

Jakob didn't see them again for six years.

30

Gentle Poverty

A QUARTER OF A MILE EAST of the village and toward the river lived a young couple with one child. A farmer let them build a one-room cabin of willow and poplar, insulated from the north winds with a plaster of cow manure, straw and earth. No documents were signed, no payment made. Perhaps, in return, the husband cleared some brush and did some chores for the farmer. With spade and hoe they planted a small garden plot. He found whatever work was available in the farming community at fifteen to twenty-five cents an hour. The big money was to be made in the threshing season at three dollars a day, from dawn to dark. In a good year, when the weather and crops were right, he could earn up to a hundred dollars a season.

On the occasional winter Sunday, Jakob found the little family a warm place to visit. He never recalled what was said in their conversations except that the man listened to a boy of twelve who had so much to say. Perhaps they shared *Prips*, a coffee-like drink made from roasted wheat. He was dimly aware of the quiet female presence in the background who swept the packed earth floor, changed diapers or nursed the cooing baby who never cried.

One day, during a pause in the conversation, the man bent down to pull a box of western pulp magazines from under the bed. A few minutes later, Jakob was absorbed in the adventures of Cactus Carrington, an honest and upright gunslinger who rode through the sage brush into the nearest town to reverse whatever wrongs needed to be righted. When he finished the story and reached for another, the husband was sound asleep.

His young wife smiled, put a finger to her lips and pointed to the sleeping child in the apple crate. Jakob shouldered his Mackinaw, stepped into his felt boots, covered his ears with the flaps of fur and pulled on his mittens. As he closed the door behind him, he heard the click of the latch slide into place.

The sun was sinking in the west. A winter glow transformed the snowdrifts into sand dunes and the willows turned to "burning sagebrush." He urged his cayuse to a gallop. He was Cactus Carrington, a 30/30 carbine in the scabbard of his saddle. As he neared the first house in the village he reined in his horse to a canter, then to a walk. No need to attract unnecessary attention. Better to surprise any outlaws hanging around the saloon, bent on mischief.

"Where did you go?" asked Mama.

"Henry Janzen's."

"And what did you do?"

"We just talked."

"They're very poor. Did you eat *Faspa?*"

"I don't remember. I don't think so."

"I'll set the table."

1932

Franklin D. Roosevelt defeats Hoover on a promise to balance the federal budget. After the election, Roosevelt meets with his advisors and decides to abandon his campaign platform to cut spending and authorizes Harry Hopkins to pump money into the economy and get people back to work. The New Deal ends the worst suffering of the Depression and gives Americans hope for the future. Under Roosevelt, the federal government created unemployment insurance, social security and some welfare.

France signs a non-aggression pact with Russia. The Swiss psychoanalyst Carl Jung calls Picasso a "schizophrenic." Germany has 30% unemployment and the Nazis become the dominant political party in the Reichstag.

In Canada, for 48 days the Schellenberg crystal set reports the pursuit of Albert Johnson, the "Mad Trapper of Rat River," who has killed one Mountie and wounded another in the high Arctic. He eludes the posse until World War I pilot Wop May, flying a single engine monoplane, finds him. Johnson is shot and killed by his pursuers.

31

Potatoes

To survive through the grasshopper years, the family planted extra potatoes, which they peddled to householders in the city. Although the field was small, to Jakob the rows of plants to be weeded, hoed and beetle-picked by hand seemed to go on forever. To control fungus, they were sprayed with Paris green—a poisonous arsenic mixture which was also used to kill grasshoppers and garden insects. In fall, they dug up the tubers with flat-pronged forks, taking care not to bruise them. City housewives expected vegetables from the farm to look perfect.

Last year Papa promised that this fall, the year of Jakob's twelfth birthday, he could try his skill at selling potatoes to the ladies in the city This would be the first time he would meet and talk to *Englaenda* by himself. All year he read the "Good Manners" column in each issue of the *Winnipeg Free Press Prairie Farmer*. He wanted to be so perfect they would never suspect that he was a Mennonite boy from Rosenheim.

The evening before, he and Papa loaded as many sacks of potatoes as the Model T Ford could hold. The next morning, Jakob climbed into the driver's seat and Papa cranked the engine. Remembering that a neighbour had broken his arm when the engine kicked the crank backwards, he set the spark lever as far back as possible so that engine wouldn't backfire. Papa spun the crank, the engine sputtered. Jakob advanced the spark lever and the engine settled into a steady rhythm. As Papa stepped on the running board to get into the driver's seat, Mama came up.

"The boys haven't had fresh fruit since Christmas. If you sell enough potatoes, will you bring back an orange or a banana for each of us?"

He chuckled. "If Jakob sells all the potatoes we'll all eat bananas."

"I'm going to sell every potato we have," said Jakob. He felt so good, so giddy.

"Be careful of your promises." Papa was cautious about such things.

Papa was also a careful driver and held the Ford at a steady twenty-five miles an hour so long as there was no traffic. When a car approached or tried to pass (which was often) or a vehicle was stopped at a side road waiting to enter the flow of traffic, Papa tensed and eased his foot off the accelerator, slowing down. Horns tooted and drivers shouted and he wondered why they were in such a hurry.

"It took six hours with a horse and buggy," he said, with satisfaction. "Now we do the twenty-five miles in a little more than an hour."

As they approached a 25 MPH sign at the city limits, he slowed to fifteen miles an hour. Half an hour later, the Model T was parked in the alley of a working-class neighbourhood.

"I'll take this side. You take the houses on that side."

As Jakob approached the back door of the first house with a pail of potatoes in each hand, he rehearsed over and over what the "Good Manners" writer had said that a gentleman would do when he spoke to a lady. At the door he set down a pail and tapped twice on the screen door. He waited but heard no sound.

"Rap on the inside door!" Papa's voice, across the alley.

Jakob pulled open the screen door to knock on the inside door when it was yanked open by a little woman with a rooster face.

"Yes?" She looked angry.

Jakob almost forgot to take off his cap, like the "Good Manners" lady had said. "Good morning, ma'am. Would you like some potatoes today?"

"Well," grudgingly, "maybe. I don't really need any. Let me look at 'em. How much?"

"Twenty-five cents a pail," he almost forgot, "Ma'am."

"Wait." She disappeared and came back. "Here's fifty-five cents. An extra nickel because you're so polite." She took both pails.

In his excitement he forgot to say "Thank you, ma'am."

Except for a snarling dog at one house and two where no one answered the door, every house took a pailful and three ladies bought two. In the first block, Jakob sold eight pails of potatoes and Papa sold three.

"How did you do it, what do you say?"

"I say 'Good morning, ma'am, would you like some potatoes today?'"

"That's all?"

How could he explain that taking off his cap would sell potatoes? Sometimes you do things even if you don't understand how they work.

"That's all I said, Papa."

They sold all the potatoes, and before they drove home Papa did something he had never done. He bought a big bagful of bananas.

32

A Visitor

THEY HAD FINISHED MILKING the cows. Jakob turned the crank to spin the cream separator as Mama tipped a pail of milk into the upper bowl. A thin runnel of cream trickled out of the upper spout and skimmed milk streamed out of the lower into separate containers.

"Now, who might that be?" Mama was at the window. "It's a Bennett buggy. Papa, go and see what they want."

Papa ambled to the window. "That's Wiens." He dragged on his coat and stepped outdoors, closing the door behind him.

"He has a boy with him. Their boys go to school with you. Do you know him?"

Jakob rose and leaned to look, maintaining the constant speed of the crank. "I've never seen him before."

"They're coming in. Now what would they want?"

Papa entered, followed by Ohmkje Wiens and a youth who looked to be about four years older than Jakob. The boy's sweater seemed familiar and Jakob recalled seeing it on a Wiens boy before it had holes on the elbows. The visitor's clothes were patched, his arms and legs too long for the jacket and pants. Why would he be visiting on a weekday when every farm boy his age was at work?

The boy's eyes swept the kitchen, pausing for a moment when something held his interest. Their eyes met and Jakob felt a moment of kinship, as if they had met some other time, some other place. He knew there were things they could talk about which others would never understand. He felt an urge, a compulsion, to say something, to reach out to this stranger.

"*Nah yo*, let us go in the *grote shtov*."

The connection was broken as man and boy followed Papa into the parlour. The parlour was special, where Papa or Mama went to read undisturbed, for formal visiting, and—when the door was closed—for serious discussions. Papa closed the door.

After the milk and cream were stored in the pantry, Jakob helped Mama take the separator apart for washing. He was drying the last piece when Papa and the visitors passed through the kitchen to the front door, talking as people do whose minds are on something other than their words. As the youth turned their eyes met and Jakob remembered the eyes of a gopher in a trap.

And then they were gone.

"Who was he? What did they want?" Mama's curiosity held a tone of anxiety.

"The boy is a distant relative of Wiens. He was one of the children that was saved from Siberia by President Hindenburg. He hasn't heard from his father or mother since they parted in Moscow five years ago. He was twelve when his father put him on the train and told him if he made it to Canada to wait for them. He may never see them again. He's alone. No family. Like so many others."

"Can't anyone do anything?" asked Mama.

"The boy has distant relatives who managed to escape to Canada. They're willing to take him in. And so would most others in the church. But he wants to go to school."

"But he's a grown man!"

"Seventeen."

"But how?" Mama asked. "Why?"

"He seems to have ideas about being a doctor or something. And, of course, nobody has money for that."

It was Sunday afternoon when a neighbour brought the news.

"They came home from church this morning and found him in the garden, the shotgun at his side. His hand still held the stick he had notched, so it wouldn't slip off the trigger."

It was said, by some, that the boy spent too much time on books. Reading, they said, messes up the brain.

33

Widow Warkentin

"JAKOB! Jakob! There's a fire at the Warkentin's." It was Mama's urgent voice. He couldn't open his eyes. They were so heavy.

"Papa and I are going now. Do you want to see it? Or stay in bed? Knals and Obraum just ran out the door. Are you coming or staying in bed? It's a big fire. Their barn is burning! And so will the house!"

The yard was littered with blankets and beds and chairs and boxes. The whole village must have been there to carry out whatever wasn't fastened to the wall or floor.

"I guess I'm lucky I didn't have the money to build like they did." Papa was speaking to the neighbour.

"I never liked the idea of building a house and barn together. Even with a *Gank* between, you can smell the manure from the barn. Especially in summer, with all the doors open. But on cold winter nights, especially with a north wind and snow, my boys grumble when they have to bundle up to feed the horses for the night." Pointing at the kitchen window, "See? The smoke is now coming into the house from the barn. It won't be long for the flames."

There was enough daylight through the window into the kitchen to see smoke curling under the door. Suddenly the door blew open and flames shot into the kitchen and smoke clouded the room.

"Better step back. He said there was a can of kerosene in the kitchen."

"Anybody know how the fire started?"

"Best guess is the oldest son started it in the hayloft."

The fire was now leaping through the roof of the house.

"It won't be long now."

"Did they get the cows and horses out?"

"Oh, yes. That's why they figure the oldest boy did it. The animals were all out before anyone saw smoke."

"He liked animals. I guess they're all like that. They can't get along with people but animals are okay."

"What's going to happen to him?"

"My guess is the Mounties will take him to the insane asylum in North Battleford tomorrow."

"Where's he now?"

"Someone said he's asleep in the granary. If he can sleep, that tells you how far gone he is."

One day a *Russlaenda* came to the village in search of a bride. He had lost his family to the violence that followed the Russian revolution in 1917 and migrated too late in life to learn a new language and the ways of an alien country. With nothing to lose, he abandoned any subtlety of intention.

"I want a woman who will offer me a bed to sleep, food to eat and wash my socks."

His description of wealth and privilege—of a honeymoon on one of several ships owned by his family down the Dnieper into the Black Sea and the blue Mediterranean, of visiting Istanbul, Athens and Crete, amused the villagers. He spoke of mansions and servants and estates. Of gardeners, carriages and footmen. The men listened in silence when he spoke of these things and, when he left, shook their heads.

Widow Warkentin needed a man to be the other half of herself. And so, after a brief meeting with the minister and a week's betrothal, they married.

She was a large woman. He was a little gray man. When he hitched the old gelding to the buggy and helped her in, the buggy sagged under her weight and the opposite side tilted up. When they drove to visit her relatives, he gripped the arm of the seat to keep from sliding against her body, leaving only one hand to hold the reins.

One evening, after supper, she was kneading bread when she saw a pencil in his hand.

"You drawing pictures? What's that? That's a funny wagon. What's it for?"

"It's a carriage. The coachman sits up front."

Jake, the village handyman who was smith, carpenter, coffin maker, barn builder, metal worker and solver of problems, offered to install a coil spring to level the buggy. The *Russlaenda* remembered his coach and coachman. Following his sketches, the blacksmith reconstructed the buggy as a carriage with the driver up front and passenger behind.

Amiably, almost cheerfully, the *Russlaenda* announced a sudden loss of hearing. It was a deep disappointment to his wife, who liked to chatter as they journeyed through the quiet countryside. But after years of loneliness she was grateful for a husband who willingly drove her wherever she wanted to go. Accustomed to life without a handyman, she made few demands on the man who had never acquired the skills of repairing a hinge or hanging a storm window.

"He seems to do a lot of thinking," she said. "With no one to talk to, sitting all by himself, I wonder if he is ever lonely when we go visiting."

But he never complained. And they lived as happily as those who measure life by the yield per acre.

34

Conductor Cooper

TWO FLASHLIGHTS AND A DOZEN EGGS ended the career of Conductor Cooper.

Olsen was served by two trains. In the morning a steam locomotive brought the mail from the big city to the south. It had at least one passenger coach, a mail coach and cars for freight and baggage. On its return, it passed through town in the late afternoon.

At noon the Skunk two-coach diesel came from the north, southbound for the city. For seventy-five cents (the price of seven dozen eggs or seven pounds of butter) villagers could take the Skunk at noon and arrive in the city in half an hour to see the doctor and return the same afternoon.

Some said Cooper, the train conductor, hated Mennonites because they wouldn't go to war. But he couldn't have been to the Great War either or he would have decorated his chest with ribbons. Dressed in his navy blue uniform with polished brass buttons, he liked to frighten old ladies with his harsh voice. He might have continued to make travel miserable for the old people of the village if it had not been for the sons of the *Englaenda* who operated the Pioneer grain elevator.

They were at the age when a boy begins to become a man. First, his voice changes. Then his father or older brother makes a slingshot for him from a forked willow branch, using rubber bands from an old inner tube and a leather pouch cut from a work glove. For ammunition, he finds round stones. Some boys got to be accurate, shooting gophers and, rarely, sparrows. Of course, if he broke a window or struck a playmate the slingshot might be taken away for a while. If it happened more than once, his father might cut up the rubber bands or chop it up with an axe.

As soon as a boy could afford to, he bought a pocket jackknife. This opened a world of possibilities. He could make a slingshot fork exactly how he wanted, make a willow whistle, or whittle and carve all manner of things from the scraps of lumber to be found on any farm.

A two-cell flashlight was more costly to buy and the batteries had to be replaced. This was often paid for with the proceeds from the sale of rabbit pelts which he caught and skinned. A few youths, including the two *Englaenda*, bought powerful five-cell lights.

One dark winter evening, the northbound Skunk pulled into the dimly lit station. Unknown to Conductor Cooper, half a dozen youths were hidden in the shadow of the freight shed. The conductor stepped out and four passengers stepped down to the station platform and drifted away. Cooper looked at his railway watch. As he opened his mouth to announce ALL ABOARD! the first egg splattered the coach behind him. That is when he made a big mistake. Turning around, he held up his lantern and glared into the gloom.

"Who did that?"

Two five-cell flashlights blinded him.

"Fire," yelled the ring leader. A dozen eggs splattered Cooper's navy blue uniform with the shiny brass buttons.

Next morning, when the steam locomotive came in from the city, two strangers stepped out of the passenger coach. One was an official of the Canadian National Railway. With him was a Mountie in full uniform, high boots, a Sam Browne belt, holster and revolver.

The railway man had been in town before. "Maybe the lumber dealer can tell us something. He's at the north end of town."

"Not a very big town."

"No more than a hundred people."

The door of the lumber office and store was open, but there was no one in sight. A few seconds later a farmer entered, apparently a customer. When he noted the waiting official and the Mountie, he suggested, "I guess George must be out back. Let's go look."

They followed him through the back door to the yard where the manager was sorting lumber. "Do you ever lose merchandise when you go out and leave the door open?" asked the Mountie.

"Never lost a thing. People here don't steal. What brings you here? Anybody in trouble?"

"What do you know about last night? At the train station."

"Is there anything I ought to know?"

The postmaster, who also ran the telephone switchboard and who might have been expected to know more, had heard what had happened but had no idea who might have done it. The teacher was more cooperative. He assembled a few parents at the schoolhouse. They hadn't seen anything unusual at the station but were glad to meet someone from the city who was interested in knowing more about Conductor Cooper. And they told him a lot the railway man didn't think to ask.

"We know who did it," confided the Mountie to the postmaster who trundled his mail cart to the train. "Everyone knows who did it. But we can't find any witnesses and the big shot from the railway doesn't seem too interested."

And that was the last they saw of Conductor Cooper.

35

Katy and Herman

UNTIL KATY WAS THIRTEEN few students noticed her. If anyone had thought to ask, which no one did, they would not have remembered anything she said, or if she ever laughed or cried. The colour of her hair or eyes, or what she wore. But when she got chubby and walked funny, they noticed.

"Quack, quack."

It was all in fun and they felt badly when she stopped coming to school. Then they forgot about her until it was whispered that she had a baby.

Her family lived at the end of the village near the river. Like everyone else they spoke *Plautdietsch* but they were different. They kept to themselves, away from neighbours or villagers. Even for pig butchering.

Soon everyone knew it was a boy. The neighbours saw a shiny car at Katy's home and were sure it was the Mounties. It was said she wouldn't tell them the name of the father.

"I guess she was too scared to tell," said a villager.

"It must have been her father."

"I always thought there was something funny about that family."

"It could have been one of her brothers."

A few weeks later everyone knew for sure who it was. Katie's father came home from the hospital limping, his arm in a sling, his face battered. And he wouldn't lay charges against the neighbour's boy who had beaten him up.

"Why don't the Mounties do something? Don't they know?"

"Sure. They're no dumber than we are. But they can't do something just because they know."

Ten years passed. It was the first day of school. The new teacher had been one of the boys who teased Katy. Now her son, Herman, was one of his thirty-five students.

"I want to place each of you in the right class. This test will help me do that. The problems start easy and get so hard that no one will finish them all. Let's see how far you get in half an hour."

Herman hardly glanced at the paper, his eyes drifted restlessly around the room. He tapped his pencil on the desk, then doodled in the palm of his hand.

Strolling around the room, the teacher paused at Herman's desk.

"Having a problem?"

The class laughed. Herman giggled.

"I did, too," said the teacher.

The laughter stopped.

"That was long ago." He slowly and deliberately scanned the faces before him, now alert and attentive. "Only a few years ago not one of you could answer these questions."

The smiles vanished.

"What you learn today, you'll know tomorrow." He picked up the pencil from the desk. "Herman, let me help you."

Herman was an arduous learner. His brow wrinkled in concentration and sometimes, as he grasped the answer, his deep sigh could be heard by all in the room.

"He's got it!" And they laughed with Herman.

In the one-room school the teacher was also the janitor. He cleaned the blackboards, carried in pails of water from the well for drinking and washing. In winter when the air became too dry, he placed a third pail on top of the furnace. And to warm up the classroom for the shivering students when they arrived, he rose early to fire up the coal-burning furnace.

One winter day, after classes were dismissed, Herman lingered at the teacher's desk.

"Yes, Herman?"

"May I carry in the water?"

Each day he stayed, or arrived early, to help with the janitor work. One weekend, without telling the teacher, he came in to sweep and oil the floor.

When Herman turned fifteen and left school, the teacher persuaded the school board to hire the youth as a part time janitor at two dollars a month, which he doubled out of his own salary.

Twenty years later the teacher, now at a different school, met the teacher who had succeeded him. The boy had been often on his mind.

"What ever happened to Herman?"

"When the schools consolidated they hired him as custodian. You should have seen his face when they offered him the job!"

"Did he ever get married?"

"He married the daughter of Stony Gerbrandt. People said a school custodian could marry much better but he said she was good enough for him. He never was ambitious. I've often wondered, with so much to overcome, how did he do it?"

"He was faithful. He knew what he could do and did it well."

€va

HER EYES WERE CLOSED, her mouth relaxed, her eager hands at rest, folded in her lap. The afternoon breeze blew a curl of hair across her faded cheek.

Jakob tensed his eyes and set his jaw. Dimly, he heard the words of the pastor interweave and overlap with other sights and sounds.

"... the innocence of childhood ... *Jakob, do you think I'm innocent? ...* let them come unto Me, for of such is the kingdom of Heaven ... *Do you think I'll go to Heaven?* ... for we are on this earth for only a little while to suffer and then we go on to eternity ... *it won't hurt anymore* ... and so if we bear our cross we will join Eva in a very short time ... *Do you think God is up there looking down on us?* ... young enough to escape the temptations of the flesh ... youthful in eternity ...."

Jakob's vision blurred and he brushed the corner of his eye with the tip of his finger to remove a speck of dust that wasn't there.

Jake makes coffins for dead people, doesn't he?

He forced himself to think about Jake at work, sanding the clear white pine, his scarred and calloused hands feeling the silk-smooth surface for imperfections. The round holes in the upper edge of the coffin to receive the pegs of the lid. He tried to think how Jake got it all to line up and fit. And how neatly Mama and the village women fitted the sleeves and ironed each pleat on the white shroud and tacked it to the inside edge of the coffin, from her waist to her feet.

He looked up at Mama beside him. Diphtheria, she had said, took Eva's life. She pushed up her gold-rimmed glasses and dabbed at her left unseeing eye with a neatly folded white handkerchief. The face of Papa, across the coffin and looking over the shoulder of Eva's father, was controlled and composed and solemn. He felt a surge of pride and comfort in his father's strength.

"... a blessing when they die young for then they do not need to suffer the anxieties of parenthood ... *my Mama calls it the morning sunshine bird* ... Eva has gone to be with God and we must now live in such a way that we will meet her there ... *Let's go home the other way ...* where there's no earthly temptation ... *That cloud looks like an angel. See the wings? ...* no suffering ... no evil ... no sin ...."

The *Forsinger* cleared his throat and opened his black hymn book. He announced the selection, inhaled deeply and began a wordless chant, his voice rising and falling. When he found the range, his mouth shaped the first word of the hymn and the black clad villagers joined in the plaintive chant of the Old Colony Church.

Two men picked up the lid and carefully placed the pegs in the holes. Women wept silently and children sobbed. Jakob compressed his lips and blinked away the blur.

Eva's four brothers, with swollen eyes and wooden faces, lifted the coffin to a buggy from which the seat had been removed. Picking up the shafts in unison, they pulled the buggy down the driveway to the village street. Eva's family, the pastor and the attending villagers—numbering about twenty adults and a few children—followed the buggy in silence to the graveyard several hundred paces down the village street.

Surrounded by a barbed wire fence and covered with weeds and the odd wildflower, the forty or fifty mounds were hardly noticeable. A passing stranger might have mistaken it for an empty lot. In the tradition of the church, the dead were consigned to the earth without gravemarkers. Few villagers knew where any but their own family members were buried. Jakob knew only that four weed-covered mounds on the west end contained the remains of his brothers and a sister but no one troubled to tell them apart. He had never asked. It didn't seem important.

But every villager knew who was buried in the northeast corner, although no one knew his name. When the village was first settled at the turn of the century, a settler fishing for sturgeon pulled the body of a man from the river. They built a coffin, held a funeral and buried him, for now he was one of them.

The grave for Eva, which measured five or six feet deep and a little less in length, had been dug by four village youths. Two round-pointed shovels stood upright in the mound of fresh-piled earth, a coil of rope between them. Two boards lay across the open grave.

"Let us pray."

In silent prayer the women tugged shawls forward over eyes, the men held hats and caps over their faces. He caught the light odour of stale perspiration from his cap, a not unpleasant smell, for it was his own. A rustle of movement, of fabric touching fabric, signaled the end of prayer.

Straddling the narrow hole at each end, two men lowered the coffin on the boards and removed the lid, placing it beside the coffin. The pastor spoke to the family in Low German and read from the Bible in High German, consigning Eva's spirit to God and her body to the earth, asking the Spirit's comfort and consolation for the family. And then the coffin was closed, the rope slung under each end, the boards removed and the plain unfinished pine slowly lowered to the bottom of the grave. The rope was released on one side and pulled out the other. A young man meticulously coiled the rope, dropped it on the ground and grasped a spade.

Ears were jarred by the scrape of metal as both shovels stabbed into the mound of earth and gravel, followed by the clatter of earth clods on pine and an outburst of weeping women and crying children. Jakob tried to swallow. His eyes brimmed.

He moved behind Mama and looked up at the flowers embroidered in the corner of her shawl. He concentrated on the individual silk threads of yellow and pink and red, skillfully blended to create the subtle shades of nature. His eyes cleared, his throat relaxed.

Now the soft thud of earth on earth replaced the drum on hollow wood. His throat tightened again and his eyes filled. He looked at the blurry ground and a tear dropped off his eyelash, missing his cheek. He raised his head and looked at the fringe of Mama's shawl, counting the strands she had knotted. The tight feeling went away.

Now they were patting the earth on the little mound, shaping the ends. They leaned on their shovels as the pastor said a benediction. The muffled sobs had stilled. The sound of a distant meadowlark carried on the afternoon breeze. A grasshopper buzzed loudly across the graveyard. Then, with murmurings of conversation, the villagers turned to leave.

He felt an overwhelming loneliness. It didn't seem right to leave Eva

... alone ... at night ... in the wind and rain and cold. No one to hold her hand when she was frightened of the storm.

He looked for Mama and saw only black pleated skirts and embroidered shawls. Then he recognized the immaculately tied silk bow of her apron over the pleats of her brocaded black skirt and embroidered roses in her shawl. He felt comfort in her nearness as he walked behind her, counting the steps back to Eva's home, losing count when he got to a hundred, or was it two hundred? And he started over and then it didn't matter because his throat was easy and his eyes were clear.

For the funeral *Faspa*, the tables were set outdoors in the shade of the farmhouse. Long planks on trestles were covered with bleached flour sacks and set with large pans of fresh buns baked by the women of the village. Bowls of white sugar lumps dotted the table. Cups and saucers and cream pitchers completed the setting. Men were served first, saucering and blowing their hot coffee. They dipped a corner of the sugar cube to soften it, nibbled it, took a bite of bun and sipped coffee from the saucer. When the coffee cooled they drank from the cup and when they had enough they turned the cup upside down in the saucer.

When the men had finished, the women took the places occupied by their husbands and the children ate last. To save dishwashing some children ate from the unwashed dishes of their elders. Seeing a spotted cup before him, Jakob cringed. A hand reached over his shoulder. It was Mama, who replaced it with with a clean one.

"My children," said a disapproving voice, "are not that fussy."

Mama was talking to a little girl and hadn't heard.

The mood was light. Low laughter, the reassuring tinkle of cups and saucers, the hiss of kettles and swelling conversation eased the load of sorrow which had changed to gentle sadness. The sounds of human life began to fill the emptiness that had engulfed the villagers an hour before. Eva's mother, who helped serve the guests, had a half smile on her lips and a hint of crinkle pinched the corners of her swollen eyes. Life in the village would continue.

"Jeff and I are going to the pasture to find some gophers." Jakob had changed to overalls, slingshot in hand.

"Make sure you have the cows in the paddock for milking." Mama looked up from her Bible.

He leaped off the porch, clearing three steps with a bound. The screen door slammed as his bare feet touched the ground. He looked around for Jeff and, pursing his lips to whistle, blew hard and short. His mouth dry, he tried again.

"Here, Jeff!"

The dog paused at the corner of the house, brown eyes alert, ears pointed, tail high and gently swaying. Jakob clapped his hands and sprinted toward the pasture gate. The dog streaked past him across the yard and through the barbed wire fence. They headed north, where the silver berries were ripe and ready.

The bluebell stems were bare, the buttercups withered, looking like any other weed. A stunted dandelion struggled to capture the last rays of the summer sun. Along the fence the yellow goldenrod announced the early days of autumn.

Jeff ran ahead to sniff gopher trails and chase sparrows while Jakob searched the ground for slingshot stones. He found a few, some flat, some round, no two alike in colour or size.

A summer-fattened gopher, cheeks full of grain, zig-zagged to its burrow, Jeff in pursuit. It disappeared into the earth. Jakob loaded his slingshot, crouched and fixed his sight on the mound of earth around the hole. He caught a slight movement of dark just above the mound. He stayed motionless. The gopher-head moved up a bit. He waited. The head rose, then the body reared on its legs. He quickly stretched the rubber bands and released the stone. Before the stone left the leather pouch the gopher dived into its hole.

Full grown gophers were cautious. Most disappeared into their burrows before Jakob or the dog saw them.

At the straw stack he sat down in the setting sun. Jeff lay down beside him, panting. He leaned back, only half aware of the clouds in the bright blue sky. And then his memory shaped her voice.

See that cloud? It looks like an angel.

He threw himself face down on the straw and spilled his grief, his shoulders shaking. Jeff whimpered, came up and licked his neck. He lashed out in fury. Jeff yelped in fright and pain. And then he hugged the dog and sobbed.

The tears ran dry. His chest felt empty, his body weak. The pain had gone.

The air was still. And then he heard them.

Ahrnk ... Ahrnk ... Ahrnk ... the faint honk of whistling swans flying south for the winter. He strained his eyes, sweeping the skies, and saw them. Fifteen black dots in V formation too high to see the motion of wings.

The cows!

He leaped to his feet and looked at his shadow. By the angle of the sun it must be six.

He looked for Jeff. In the distance he saw a movement. A touch of light moving about, right and left, among the silver berry bushes a quarter-mile away. Sniffing gopher trails.

He whistled sharply. The movement stopped. He whistled again. Now the movement was up and down, faster, coming closer. Jakob sprinted for home. Halfway, Jeff caught up with him and lunged at his legs, almost knocking him to the ground. He threw a stick high in the air. Jeff leaped to catch it and ran off to the paddock where the cows were waiting to be milked.

He opened the gate and saw Mama coming down the path from the house, milk pails in hand, two cats trailing. They passed each other at the hen house.

"If you're hungry there's *borscht* on the stove."

37

The Eye

"THE DOCTOR TOLD MY PAPA if they didn't take out his bad eye he would go blind in both eyes. After the operation they gave him a glass eye but he never wore it. He said it was uncomfortable." Mama's eyes looked far away, to another time. "We should have buried it with him. But I forgot. Now I don't know what to do with it."

The Eye was kept in a Dodd's Kidney Pill box on the top shelf of the china cabinet. By standing on a chair, Jakob could open the glass door and reach it. As he slowly unwrapped the fluffy white cotton and met the glassy gaze of Grandpa, he got a funny feeling that somebody was spying on him. It got into different parts of his head and sometimes a man appeared in his dreams staring with one eye. But he didn't tell anyone about dreams or thoughts he couldn't understand.

He dimly remembered Mama's father. He'd never seen him smile. Mama didn't often speak of him except to say he was very strict. When he came home from the field, dinner had to be on the table as soon as he walked in the door. When Unkel Wellm was sixteen he ran away to Oregon, he said, to escape the beatings. He described Grandpa in words that even the village boys didn't use.

Jakob liked Unkel Wellm, even though he'd only seen him once when he came to visit. He had a beautiful shiny car and he dressed like an *Englaenda* in a suit and tie. When he had discovered that Jakob would like to play the violin, he'd said he wasn't playing his fiddle any more and if Jakob would pay for the cost of shipping, he could have it. But Jakob had no money and Papa said no.

In the busy season Helen came back to help with the farm chores.

She was fun to tease.

"I bet you don't know what I have in my hand."

"A frog? I know you're trying to scare me but I'm not afraid of anything you can hold in your hand."

She was half laughing as she bent close to look. He snapped open his hand and the Eye stared at her. She screeched like she'd been bitten by a spider. For the rest of the day she didn't answer any questions.

It was a long day.

In the two-room house everything was in its place. Mama or Papa never needed to tell him to put things back where he found them. That was the way it was and everyone did it. Each of the four brothers had his own drawer in Mama's bureau for the toys and treasures that boys collect. Everyone knew the rule; no one must open anyone else's drawer. If anyone had done so, he couldn't tell anyone else and that's the same as not looking, because the fun of knowing secrets is to tell others what you know.

Of all their visitors, Jakob most dreaded five-year-old cousin Yasch from the city who chased the hens, pulled the tail of the cat, interrupted adults when they were talking, screamed when he couldn't have what he wanted and touched the food on the table with dirty hands. When he was told to stay away from the bureau of drawers, it became the only thing that interested him.

One summer Sunday, Jakob was playing with the Eye and was about to put it back in the box when the family of his cousin drove onto the farmyard. He hesitated, then ran to the bureau, opened his drawer and carefully placed it in the very centre, staring up. He closed the drawer and sat down to look at the Eaton's catalogue. And waited.

When his cousin came in and saw that Jakob was busy, he ran straight for the bureau, grabbed the drawer handle and pulled.

With a howl of terror he fled into the kitchen. Jakob quickly slipped the Eye into his pocket, closed the drawer and was studying the catalogue as Mama and Aunt Marie entered the room.

"What happened? Did Yasch get hurt? "

"No. I just showed him Grandpa's eye and he screamed."

Jakob took it out of his pocket, tilting it so that Yasch could see it. He bawled, sniveled and whimpered into Aunt Marie's skirt.

"Put it away," said Mama. As they left the room she gave Jakob a look and a twinkle that knew more than she said.

Many years later, when Mama had only a few weeks to live, she was reminiscing with Jakob about her childhood. She spoke of her father and she remembered his glass eye.

"I wanted to bury it with him. I forgot." Her voice and eyes spoke the guilt of a neglected duty.

"Would you like it to be buried with you?"

"Yes," she brightened and smiled. "That would be nice."

And so the Eye was placed in her coffin.

At her feet. ·

38

The Whiffletree

PAPA GRASPED THE TOP of the rear wagon wheel and rocked.

"It needs grease."

"How can you tell?"

He grasped a front wheel, pulled and pushed.

"Listen."

Jakob heard a faint sucking sound.

"That's the sound of grease. Now try the back wheel again."

Jakob pulled and pushed. He heard the click of metal on metal.

"Dry as a bone. We'll grease them all."

Loosening the lock nut, Papa pulled out the wheel to expose the dry shaft. The boy dipped a paddle into the grease bucket and generously smeared the shaft. Papa pushed back the wheel and locked it. He laid a sturdy hand on the steel rim.

"The rim is beginning to creep off the wheel. If it comes off on the road into town, the wheel will fall apart, the axle will drop to the ground, break the wagon box and spill the grain. I'd have to walk back with the team, hitch them to another wagon, salvage whatever grain we could, then load the broken pieces of wheel on the wagon and work a week to put it together and— Well, you see what happens if we don't fix things before they break. Get me a mallet from the shop."

He hammered the rim into place.

"What makes it come off?"

"The oak dries up and shrinks. The wheel gets smaller and the rim expands. Avoid driving on stony ground if you can. Pounding on rocks with a heavy load is like hammering on an anvil. That's how I expand the metal on the plowshares when they wear down. I hammer them, metal on metal."

"What do we do now?"

"We swell the oak. The wheel gets bigger to fill the rim."

From pails of water filled at the well, they splashed each wheel until all the oaken parts were wet.

Swinging hand scoops, Knals and Jakob took most of the afternoon to load the wagon with wheat. Papa would haul the load to town in the morning.

Overnight the heavy load had sunk the wagon wheels into the soft earth.

"We should have moved it to harder ground. It won't be easy for two horses to pull the wagon out of the hollows, four wheels at the same time. Especially with that load," observed Papa. "That's about sixty bushels."

Obraum hitched the big gray and the spirited bay. "Let me do it."

Papa hesitated. His short-tempered second son had more accidents than he should, especially with animals. Last year a runaway broke the hitch on the buggy. This was not the season to repair harnesses or fix wagons. But how would the boy learn without experience?

"I don't want any broken harnesses," warned Papa.

Obraum flushed, as he did when angry. He snatched the reins from Jakob, stepped on the hub of the wheel and swung up on the buckboard seat.

"Giddap!" he yelled, and whipped the reins.

The startled gray leaped forward. Leather traces snapped taut, swivelling the whiffletree, throwing the bay off balance.

"Giddap!" He lashed the bay.

The startled horse bounded forward. The whiffletree reversed and yanked the gray on its haunches. Obraum shook out the loose ends of the reins.

"Stop!" Papa waved his hand.

Obraum lowered the reins. "The load's too heavy," he growled. "The horses can't do it. We'll have to unload."

"What would you do?" Papa turned to Jakob.

"Can I try?"

Papa nodded.

"Snot nose," muttered Obraum, throwing down the reins.

The horses were heaving, breathing heavily and stomping restlessly.

"Will you hold the reins, Papa?"

Jakob stepped in front of the horses, their heads high, nostrils flaring, ears erect, anxious and alert.

"Easy, easy," he murmured.

He slowly reached out to stroke their muzzles and forelocks, continuing to speak in low and reassuring tones.

"Dumb. Talking to horses like they were people," mumbled Obraum.

Their necks slowly relaxed, their heads gradually lowered, hooves stilled and breathing eased. A deep sigh.

Jakob grasped the bridles, backed up and urged them forward.

"Come!"

The traces tightened. The gray, eager to follow Jakob, was ahead of the bay. Jakob pushed back, lightly but firmly, and watched the gray relax. He tugged at the bridle of the bay. Both were leaning into harness now, whiffletrees straight, traces taut.

"Come!" In a sharp voice.

He quickly stepped back with a strong pull on both bridles. Eight muscular legs strained. The wagon creaked and swayed. Four wheels turned and rolled up and out onto level ground.

"Would you like to take the load to the elevator?"

Papa's question took Jakob by surprise. At this time of year Papa always hauled the grain to the elevator himself, where he closely questioned the buyer about quality and grade. And he met farmers from other villages to hear news of auction sales, the outlook for the crops and the weather.

"Don't forget to pick up the mail." Papa's eyes twinkled a bit, like they did before he laughed. Which he didn't.

39

The Cat's Whisker

THE CAT'S WHISKER was magic. It was the point of a fine, coiled wire with which Jakob probed and picked at the crystal to find the best reception of a radio station on a crystal set made by Knals. The receiver was assembled from five pieces: a wire wrapped around a paper tube, a condenser that resembled a piece of chocolate candy, a little piece of crystal wrapped in lead, a cat's whisker and a two-dollar set of headphones which Knals separated so both could listen at the same time.

"Where does the power come from?"

"I guess nobody knows," said Knals. "Maybe from the sun. Or the crystal. It just works. That's all I know."

When he heard Foster Hewitt describe a live hockey game on Saturday night, Jakob felt like he was at the Maple Leaf Gardens.

"Here come Apps, Drillon and Davidson down centre ice. Apps has the puck, passes to Davidson who passes to Drillon and back to Apps.

He shoots, he scores!"

On cold winter evenings the crystal set could bring in KSL, Salt Lake City and the Mormon Tabernacle Choir with Richard Evans in his unforgettable deep voice "from the crossroads of the West, music and the spoken word."

"What's a Mormon?"

"I don't know. But they sure can sing."

"I met Henry Fischer at the elevator today. He has a radio for sale, an Atwater Kent. A real radio. Five dollars. I'm going over to Hochschtedt tomorrow to have a look. You want to come, Jakob?"

The following afternoon they hitched a team of horses to a sleigh on which Papa and Knals had built a cabin and installed a wood-fired heater. The crystal set had forecast a cold evening with a north wind, about thirty below. They would need the heater for the return trip.

An hour and a half later, they arrived on the farmyard of the Fischers, the horses steaming, their nostrils crusted with frost. Henry helped unhitch the team and directed them to stalls in the stable.

"We'll water them before you go home."

The attic where Henry slept was crowded with coils of wire, bulbs, dismantled radios, electrical gear and strange-looking parts that Jakob had never seen before. Hung from the ceiling by a cord was a light bulb that constantly dimmed and brightened.

"That's powered by my wind charger on the roof. When the wind picks up it gets brighter and when it dies, so does the light. Okay, let's try the radio. Sorry, Jakob. I can connect only one headset which I'll share with your brother. Can you find something to read? There's a pile of stuff over there."

People often spoke of Henry being different, reading stuff that others didn't. Now Jakob could be alone with whatever Henry liked to read. One stack was *Popular Mechanics* and *Popular Science* magazines. Another was a mix of periodicals and papers.

A headline caught his attention. JOBS FOR EVERYONE!

Germany's economy was strong. National Socialist Party of Germany. Everyone was working. Nobody going hungry. Hitler wants peace. New construction going up everywhere. No beggars in the street. Hitler orders Dr. Porsche to design a people's car that anyone could afford. A bug-like car with an engine in the back. A family stands hand-in-hand beside a new Volkswagen in front of a freshly painted house. There are pictures of happy school children in new clothes. Education is free for everyone. Busy factories, work camps for youth, high speed autobahns, bridges, streamlined diesel electric trains. Except for the funny-looking car it all made sense. One of his uncles had often said it could be done. Now someone had done it.

On the sleigh ride home, with the heater fired up and the horses finding their own way without direction, they both dozed off. After a while, Jakob awoke and looked at the moon. The moon that would shine on all the unemployed people in the West. And on the people, hard at work, in Germany.

"Knals, do you think that Hitler will—someday—be our leader?"

But Knals was asleep. Like many others.

40

A New Suit

IN SPRING, when the last snow was gone, the bishop conducted a ceremony of baptism for the dozen villages in the settlement. It was a coming-of-age ritual and any youth not baptized by the age of twenty-one was a suspected *Daugenix*, a good-for-nothing.

"I think Jakob should come to church with us this year to see the baptism. But he has outgrown his jacket and pants." Mama liked everyone in the family to look nice. When Papa's serge suit began to show a tinge of red in the sunlight she urged him to replace it. When he didn't, she bought pinstripe navy blue worsted and made a whole suit for him on her Singer machine.

"Can we buy Jakob a new suit?"

"If we find a good navy blue serge at the right price." That meant going to the city. "We'll go to Lehrer's first, then to Adelman's." He cautioned Jakob, "If Lehrer or Adelman shows us a suit that you like very much, don't let him know. If he sees you want it he won't bargain on the price."

To avoid the traffic, Papa parked the Model T in the Eaton's parking lot and they walked across the footbridge over the railway tracks to the Jewish stores on the west side.

Mr. Lehrer shook hands with Papa and slapped the boy on the shoulder, which grownup people in Rosenheim would never do, Jakob thought.

"The boy needs a suit," said Papa.

"I got a deal for you, Mr. Schellenberg." He took a tweedy-looking suit from the rack. "See the tag? It's a thirty-five dollah suit and you can have it for half price. Seventeen-fifty."

"Navy blue serge." Papa was firm. "No more than ten dollars."

"Navy blue? I got just the suit for you, young man. Here, try this one. Yes, the sleeves are a little long but you'll grow into them. Price? You wouldn't believe, Mr. Schellenberg. Only nineteen ninety-nine. To you, my favourite customer, sixteen-fifty."

"Ten dollars."

"You drive me out of business, Mr. Schellenberg." He turned to Jakob. "Your father's a hard man, boy. He jews me down every time he comes. He'll bankrupt me." Turning to Papa, "Okay, fifteen dollah."

"Take the coat off, Jakob. We go to Adelman's across the street. If he doesn't give us a better deal we'll come back."

Outside, as they turned up the street, Jakob turned anxiously to Papa. "Will he really go bankrupt? Will we drive him out of business?"

Papa pointed to the sign in the window.

CLOSING OUT SALE! EVERYTHING MUST GO!

"So he's going out of business anyway?"

"That sign was there last year," chuckled Papa. "And it will be up again next year."

"Mr. Schellenberg, Mr. Schellenberg!" Breathing hard, Mr. Lehrer caught up with them, the suit over his arm. "Twelve dollah. But don't tell anyone. They will laugh at me for selling a quality suit so cheap. What do you say? Twelve dollah?"

"I think I paid too much," said Papa, as they drove home. "I should have offered him ten-fifty."

41

Baptism

ON THE BAPTISMAL SUNDAY morning, Jakob polished Papa's Sunday boots and Mama's shoes. She laid out her best undergarments, made of fine white cotton salvaged from sacks that had once contained salt and sugar. She shrugged into a white *Schnieawest*, tightly fitted to flatten and conceal her breasts. Over the loose white crinoline she pulled an ankle-length pleated skirt of brocaded black cotton. A matching blouse, pleated to conceal any curve or form, was buttoned to the neck. She tied the satin ribbon of a black apron in a large bow at the back and a lace-and-ribbon bonnet on her head. A shawl of fine black cotton with hand-tied fringe completed her formless and dramatic image of black. When she turned, the contrast of vividly embroidered flowers on the black shawl struck the eye.

Papa dressed in his store-bought navy blue shirt with buttoned collar and his pinstriped suit. Jakob wore his navy suit and white shirt and wished he could wear a tie.

"Are any of the Klassen girls from Reinland to be baptized this year?"

"I don't think so."

"They are so good at memorizing. Last year their Anna was able to perfectly recite all one hundred and ninety-nine catechism answers. Her mother was so proud."

"Did she get married?"

Mama laughed. "Yes, to one of the Neudorf boys from Hochschtedt. Her father didn't think much of that church. For baptism they memorized only sixty-five answers. Some people make so much of so little."

"I wonder if she understood what she memorized?" said Papa.

Neuanlage lay nine miles northwest from Rosenheim, a half hour drive for the Model T, Papa at the wheel. When they arrived there were some twenty horse-drawn vehicles, including Bennett buggies, democrats and one or two four-wheeled cabriolets with folding tops.

Tall for his age, this year Jakob was allowed to scale the outside ladder to see the ceremony from the church attic with half a dozen youths in their teens and twenties. A large trapdoor had been opened to ventilate the sanctuary below, around which the youths gathered to observe the rites and make irreverent comments.

The women sat to the left of the centre aisle, men to the right. Ten female baptismal candidates sat on the front bench of the women's section. Dressed in dark pleated dresses and black aprons, the hair of seven had been severely pulled back into a plain or plaited knot. The other three, having confessed to a loss of virginal virtue, wore black fringed and embroidered shawls tied under the chin, like married women.

"Who did it?"

"Hendrick Dyck, the *Schlingel*. Third from right." He pointed to the bench in front of the male congregation.

"How do you know?"

"Everybody knows. Anyway, boys don't have to wear anything special, but they should have tied a red ribbon to the button of his fly."

Hendrick was no *Schlope-metz*. He came from energetic stock. His father bought produce from local farmers which he sold or traded in the city at a modest profit. It was rumoured that his wife forced him to retire after he had made a deal with a city housewife which included an infection. His wife, a caring and nurturing woman, convinced him to retire from his exhausting activities. The villagers agreed that his son promised to be a worthy successor.

The *Forsinger*, who sat with the *Ohms* on an elevated bench facing the congregation, opened a hymn book and loudly cleared his throat. The congregation took the cue. When the coughing settled, he started to sing the first syllable, realized it was too high and started lower, sliding up and down until his search was successful. With confidence he attacked the second syllable and the congregation, finding the range, joined in. One nasal voice, with the piercing quality of a nail on a sheet of galvanized roofing, rose over all the others. Jakob traced it to a woman sitting behind Mama, who squirmed whenever the congregation struck a high note.

Bishop Loeppky conducted the baptism. He was Papa's cousin and when he came to Rosenheim to preach in the old schoolhouse, he usually came for lunch. When the bishop shook hands with Jakob and said, "Gondach," Jakob felt he was in the presence of God. His white hair, clear blue eyes, clean shaven and kindly face conveyed a feeling of warmth. Dressed severely in black, his trousers were tucked into polished slip-on riding boots, the tops of which met the bottom of his knee-length dress coat. His resonant voice and clear words added distinction to an already impressive appearance.

Jakob once heard an uncle say if Loeppky had been bishop at the time, Grandpa would never have been excommunicated.

Jakob looked around the attic. Stacked along the walls were pails of lard, hundred-pound bags of flour and smaller sacks of sugar and salt. From the rafters hung one or two smoked hams and three rolls of bacon.

He now remembered the attic was a food bank for the needy. He recalled Papa telling Mama when he returned from a church brotherhood meeting, that the "attic" was running low and he had agreed to supply a sack of flour.

42

Omkje Wieler

OMKJE WIELER, the general storekeeper, was a canny man. A man of kindly wit and humour, he was much appreciated by the villagers and farmers of the settlement who came in with eggs, butter and produce to exchange for groceries. He couldn't accept everything they offered and when he did, couldn't always give as much in value as they hoped. But whether he declined or bartered, they smiled when they left his store.

Mrs. Harder lived down by the river where the saskatoon berries grew wild on the bushes of the riverbank. They were now in season and she brought a pailful to the store.

"A dollar-fifty?" she asked.

"Seventy-five cents," answered Wieler.

"Then I'll sell them to the housewives in town. I can get more."

"You should put them in a nice container. They will look better. Here's one. You can return it after you sell them." He held out a new chamber pot which hadn't been selling. Mrs. Harder had never seen one.

"That's pretty. It has a cover, too. I'll wash it before I bring it back." Wieler smiled.

She came back when the store closed.

"I didn't sell a single berry. But they all wanted to know where I got the pot with the nice flowers painted on the outside."

"I'll buy your berries. At your price."

And he sold all the chamber pots on hand to the town's people. At least, that was the story and everyone believed it because Omkje Wieler was a canny man, as he demonstrated on another occasion when Mrs.

Penner entered the store with several pounds of butter.

"Overnight a mouse fell in the cream and drowned before I had a chance to make it into butter. I took the mouse out and, well, this is the butter. I don't want to sell it, but would you please exchange it for someone else's butter? Someone else would never know about the mouse and what they don't know won't hurt them."

"You are so right, Mrs. Penner."

He took her butter into the storage room, wrapped it in wax paper and returned it to her.

"Oh thank you, Omkje Wieler, everybody says that you are so helpful."

And canny.

43

A Good Doctor

AT THIS TIME OF YEAR Papa looked for clear and sunny skies for the grain to ripen, be cut, stooked, threshed and safely stored in bins. If rain fell on the ripening grain, the weight could collapse the stems and many kernels could be lost. If it drizzled for two or three days after the crop was stooked, it would get a lower grade at the elevator and sell for much less. At worst, a rain at harvest time could ruin everything the family had worked for all year.

Jakob saw it differently. When, half asleep in the early morning, he heard the patter of drops he knew there would be no stooking that day. He rolled over and snuggled under the blanket. He would sleep in that morning.

In summer, as the fields of wheat and oats and rye turned from green to golden ripe, the *Binga* was readied to reap the harvest. With a hammer on the anvil, Jakob pounded the old rivets out of the sickle, replaced the knives and hammered in eighty new rivets. The forward edge of the elevator canvas was reinforced with new material. Bearings were checked, bolts tightened and finally, the knotter was adjusted. Only Papa knew how to make the knotter do its magic. Shaped like the beak of an eagle, the two parts grasped the twine, tied it securely around a sheaf of grain and cut it. Many times Jakob tried to tie a knot with one hand. Though he had twice as many fingers as the knotter, he could never do it without using the other hand.

"How can it tie a knot with only a beak, like a bird?"

Papa chuckled. "Look carefully while I turn it, slowly."

Though Jakob watched closely, he could never see how it was done.

Except for the knotter, he understood how all the other parts of the *Binga* worked together. The horses pulled it forward, turning the big wheel which drove a chain which turned the wooden blades that pushed the grain stalks against the sickle driven by a pitman. Rollers moved the canvas which lifted the grain stalks to the tilting board where revolving rakes packed the bundles of grain for tying and knotting. He could follow all of it, except the knotter.

After the sheaves were tied and dropped on the carrier, Knals, seated up high, used a foot pedal to lower them in rows on the ground, in groups of four or five.

It was a hot day. Just right, Papa said, for harvesting. Who could tell how long the weather would last?

At breakfast, Obraum complained that Knals was favoured again. It wasn't fair, he said. Why couldn't he drive the *Binga*? Each season Papa explained he could not take the risk of a runaway team smashing up the machine. Obraum was ever in a hurry and, if the machine clogged up, he would not take time to unhook the traces. If the team spooked as he cleared the elevator canvas, the sickle would chop off his legs above the ankle. Each harvest it happened to someone, somewhere. The farm was a dangerous place and Papa was a cautious man.

"Giddap!" Knals snapped the bamboo whip at the flank of the lagging gray gelding on the right and the team surged forward. As the machine passed a row, he lowered the carrier and five sheaves dropped on the ground.

Jakob hated stooking. Maybe it was Obraum he despised. "Let's get to work." Always bossy. "Lots to do. Here, I'll start a stook. You can finish it." Obraum took one sheaf in each hand, plunked them down on the stubble so they stood up, leaning against each other. "Little snots can't do that. But at least you can pick up one at a time and stack two or three against those two. C'mon now, get to work!"

It would be another hot day. Hot days made Jakob sick in the stomach. Especially when stooking. The stubble poked under his pant legs, scratched his ankles. Thorns of Russian thistle fell in his boots.

An hour later, Knals completed a circle of the field. Jakob ran to meet the *Binga* and, as the machine went by, grabbed the crock of water from the platform. The horses, anticipating a rest, lagged. Knals snapped the whip. "Giddap!" Jakob pulled the cork, raised the crock and gulped the warm water.

"Gimme that." Obraum took a long draught and returned the crock to Jakob. By now, the *Binga* was too far away. He corked the crock and placed it in the shade of a stook where Knals would pick it up on the next lap.

"I feel sick," Jakob retched.

"But there's nothing coming up."

"I'm going to lie down for a while. In the shade." He pulled a sheaf from the stook for a pillow and lay down.

"I think you don't want to work," mumbled Obraum. "Always, I have to do it by myself."

"You think he's sick?" Papa sounded doubtful.

Mama rolled a ball of dough and tucked it next to another on the bread pan. "We need a few things from town. Why don't you talk to Dr. Hamm?"

"The doctor says you are to take a tablespoon of this medicine every morning until the stomachache goes away. It won't taste good but good medicine never does. Here, take it."

When Papa said to do something, somebody did something.

Jakob spat and spat. He drank water and spat some more. The taste didn't go away until he had some bread and jam at midmorning.

On Sunday, Unkel Johann and Tante Tina came to visit. The men cracked sunflower seeds and, sometimes, spoke about the weather and the harvest. And other things.

"You know, Hamm is a very good doctor."

"How?" asked Unkel Johann.

"Those stomach bitters he prescribed for Jakob. One tablespoon and it fixed his stomach. No more stomach sickness."

"He says the young doctors are better educated."

Papa spat a sunflower shell.

"But do they know as much?"

44

Unkel Hein Returns

WHEN HE WAS TOLD they would be coming, Jakob wasn't sure what to do if she were to hug him. That thought vanished when he saw her.

The beautiful bride had turned fat! Her chin was now a pair of double jowls. The auburn hair scented with flowers was covered by a shawl like Mama's. Even her voice, once melodic, had changed to a boisterous one. This bride of Unkel Hein who had stirred him as a boy now looked like any other Old Colony *Mumkje*.

They had three children, a little boy and two preschool girls with long braids and dresses buttoned from neck to ankle; they looked like little *Mumkjes*.

Unkel Hein wore no necktie, his shirt had no collar which, he said, was an unnecessary adornment. Collarless shirts not being available, his wife sewed his shirts. At *Faspa* he talked much about the Sabbath.

"I never shave on Sunday, not even to go to church. That would be labour, which we are forbidden on that holy day. I shave on Saturday, and make sure I do it before midnight."

Papa said nothing. Not even about the car bumpers that had been painted black.

As quickly as *Faspa* was over, Jakob escaped. He wanted to keep the memory of a warm hug and the aroma of that day six years ago when Unkel Hein and his beautiful bride left for Sonningdale.

45

Mr. Wenger

AT NINE IN THE MORNING fifty students, Grades 1 to 8, assembled in the one-room schoolhouse. Because everyone knew about the strap in the drawer of the teacher's desk, most were well-behaved. But Henry, an older student in Grade 8, always tested new teachers. When Mr. Wenger started his first day, Henry whispered to the girl in front of him and when the teacher stared at him Henry pretended not to notice, even when the teacher said there would be no talking in class.

"I'm not going to warn anyone again."

The next day after morning recess, Henry whispered to his neighbour and laughed loud enough for everyone to hear.

"I warned you! Out!" Mr. Wenger pointed to the cloakroom. He yanked open the desk drawer, took out the strap and followed Henry.

"Hold out your hand," came his voice over the wall. The girls turned pale as the sound of leather struck flesh.

When Papa asked Mr. Wenger why he left a big city to come to a little Mennonite settlement, Mr. Wenger said his ancestors were Mennonites and he wanted to live the old Mennonite ways that everyone in United States had forgotten. But the Wengers didn't live like villagers. He wore a necktie and Mrs. Wenger wore lipstick and cut her hair and they never went to the Old Colony church in the village or came to pig butchering. Maybe because nobody invited them.

When Mr. Wenger asked the school board if he could teach Sunday school in summer and would they get him a piano or organ to play hymns, they said okay but only if it didn't cost anything. A few *Russlaenda* from the farms around the village came. Jakob came because

Hedda, the teacher's daughter, the only girl with short hair, had given him an I-love-you card on Valentine's Day. That year he failed the spring exams so he could stay in the same class with Hedda.

When he taught Sunday school Mr. Wenger was sad. And he made everyone else sad. He described how they made Jesus suffer for their sins and how they were all miserable sinners and anyone who didn't feel bad about the evil things they did would burn forever in Hell. He cried and said the hardhearted who didn't cry would never be saved. Jakob tried hard to cry but couldn't remember any sins except that he played with it when he shouldn't. Another time he accidentally bent the gold-plated nib on Papa's fountain pen. But even worse had been when he did it in his pants. He was four years old but had really cried with shame over that. Maybe old men like Mr. Wenger had bigger or more sins to repent. After three classes he gave up and quit Sunday school. He missed Hedda but knew he would see her again on Monday.

That Christmas, Mr. Wenger gave each boy a necktie even though everyone knew that wearing a necktie was wrong.

"Maybe we pay him too much," said Papa.

"How much?" asked Mama.

"Five hundred a year and he works only nine months."

When people whispered that Mr. Wenger was too friendly with the girls in Grade 7 and 8 and sometimes tickled them to make them giggle, the school board called a meeting and asked him questions. They explained that California might be different but Old Colony men don't touch young girls. A week later they got a letter from his lawyer.

This started a lot of talk in the village. It was the first time the big boys asked questions of the little boys and Jakob told them everything they wanted to hear. Next day, a friendly member of the school board asked him about Mr. Wenger and the girls. He smiled when Jakob told him of a time when Mr. Wenger rang the bell to end recess and the students raced each other into the classroom. Everyone was flushed and out of breath and the teacher put his hand on the chest of a girl in Grade 8 and said, "Oh my. Your heart is beating so fast."

Jakob had forgotten about it until the trustees paid for his train ticket to the city and for his supper at a Chinese café. The meeting with the lawyers was fun ... it was a game in which the lawyers tried to trip him up. But it was easy when he pictured in his mind what he had seen and described it exactly as it had happened. When they said he would be questioned by other lawyers who would try to confuse him, he began to look forward to the day in court but was disappointed when he was told it was over. Mr. Wenger had dropped the lawsuit. And Hedda wouldn't talk to him 'til the end of the term when her father resigned.

Many days later, when Papa and one of the trustees were talking, Jakob overheard what the lawyer had said:

"That young man will go far."

Far? Where?

Part
four

1935

The heart-lung machine is invented. Radar is developed. Elvis Presley is born and Will Rogers drowns in a float plane. Mussolini invades Ethiopia. Hitler denounces the Treaty of Versailles. Franklin Roosevelt signs the U.S. Social Security Act.

One of every 10 Canadians lives on welfare. From British Columbia, 800 unemployed men board freight trains bound for Ottawa to complain. They are stopped in Regina and their leaders arrested. Four days later they are forced onto trains and taken to "work camps."

"The apples of British Columbia rot on the ground, the salmon from the Pacific and the cod from the Atlantic are plowed under fields because we do not have the money to buy our own food. Where is money when we need it? Like the topsoil on the farms it has drifted into places where it no longer supports life!" On his promise to issue a monthly dividend of $25 to every father, mother and child, Alberta voters elect William Aberhart as premier.

The federal government grants the Bank of Canada exclusive rights to print money.

Jakob is 13.

46

Ditzied-Yantzied

THIS SIDE-THE OTHER SIDE. Half a mile east of the village the river snakes a winding groove through the prairie. From the street a villager saw a road, a thin line, up the far side of the river ascend the slope to merge with the distant skyline four or five miles away. On mornings when the air shimmered in the summer sun, a mirage of houses and trees rose over the horizon, only to vanish when the sun warmed the earth. On a clear day in summer, the bright gold of the setting sun bounced off the windows across the river.

Yantzied, a mysterious place.

The *Yantzieda* were said to be different from *Ditzieda*. They spoke a funny *Plautdietsch*. Papa said they dropped the "en" to save time and time is money. "They go too much mit the world," he added. "When they come to visit, they knock on your door like an *Englaenda* instead of just walking in. Pretentious."

Ditzieda Old Colonists believed in the simple, uncomplicated and unadorned. Ritual, revelry, celebration, festivity, games, pomp, amusement, entertainment, card playing, music and dancing were unseemly and bordered on sinfulness. Lacy curtains served no purpose except to show off. Christmas trees especially were symbols of paganism and, when a candle at a *Yantzied* Christmas program ignited the tree and turned the school to ashes, there were rumours of divine retribution. The pursuit of education, fun and merriment was a challenge to divine authority. They recalled Genesis and The Fall, when Adam and Eve, too curious for knowledge, were evicted from Paradise and doomed to a future of work, sweat and pain.

Yantzieda joked that *Ditzieda* believed anything enjoyable to be a sin. *Ditzieda* suspected *Yantzieda* of believing every sin to be fun.

A *Yantzied* man, already twenty-eight and not yet married, bought a secondhand Model T Ford with glass windows. At the Salvation Army store he bought a pair of white shoes, a little too big for him, but good as new. On Saturday, he took the ferry at Clark's Crossing to show off his china-cabinet-on-wheels to the girls on *Ditzied*. He might have succeeded in goodness-knows-what, had it not been for the white shoes, which alarmed any village girl not born yesterday. However, a teacher at a nearby school, new from the city and not so alert, got in the family way by him and, before it showed, married a robust farm boy.

To explore possibilities where he was not so well known, the man from *Yantzied* decided to look for girls in another village, farther away. Removing the cap on the gas tank to check the fuel level, he struck a light for a better look. He only survived four painful days in the hospital. Long enough, they solemnly said, to make things right with God.

The elders shook their heads. *"Ach, daut es obah yaumalich met de Yantzieda!"* [3]

As Jakob's voice changed and his hair grew in new and interesting places, he sometimes found it better to act without permission because Papa didn't like to make a decision that was different from one he made the year before. It was New Year's Eve and Jakob had an invitation to celebrate.

"Don't be anxious if I come home very late tomorrow morning."

"With good people?"

"Oh, yes." It was best not to mention they were crossing the river.

"Will there be dancing?"

"I don't know." He didn't. Not for sure. Not absolutely.

"Pauss mau up," [4] the elder warned. They both knew he meant more than he said.

As seven teenagers set out on the bobsled behind two stout work horses, the setting sun tinted the snowscape with amber and laid long shadows between the dunes. The temperature dropped, the breath of animal and man turned to fog. The air, cold enough to bite lungs, slowed the team to a steady walk.

The sleigh crunched and creaked on the snow-packed trail to the shoreline, overgrown with willows and saskatoon berry bushes, over the ice and up the *Yantzied* bank. A full moon sparkled the snow and edged the clouds with light as they drifted across the star-strewn sky. The

[3] "Tsk, it's a shame about these people from the other side!"
[4] "Be careful."

young couples, without complaint, snuggled together for warmth in the crisp cold of the night. Occasionally they broke into carols from Christmas school programs: "*Stille Nacht, Heilige Nacht*" [5] and "Hark the Herald Angels Sing."

Two hours later they pulled into the farmyard of their host. Even before they stopped, the front door of the house opened to release a flood of light and warmth. Quickly the horses were unhitched and chomping fresh hay in a warm barn.

George, the eldest son of the family, showed them around.

"The outhouse will be cold tonight. We'll hang kerosene lanterns in the barn. The girls can use the cow barn. It's separated with bales of straw from the horse stalls where the fellows can go. There's lots of newspapers at each end."

They had thought of everything! And how different were the *Yantzieda* parents, who welcomed their young guests to deposit their winter coats in their bedroom, and served mugs of warm cherry wine and hot coffee. From the next room came the sounds of fiddle and banjo, and the tap and shuffle of feet. The party was already in motion.

"Hey, Jakob. I hear you play the fiddle. How about giving me a rest?"

They cheered and clapped. "C'mon, Jake!"

He felt warm and embarrassed. They put the fiddle in his hand. Encouraged, he struck the first note of "Turkey in the Straw," which was immediately picked up by the banjo player whose *pickety-pock* drowned out the scratch of his bow. As the laughter and chatter and tempo of dancing increased, the carefree mood eased his anxiety. To his surprise, the scraping sound of the bow at the beginning of each stroke had disappeared.

After hours of dancing and snacking on *Zwieback* and coffee, the hosts helped to hitch the horses. Rested, fed and watered—impatient to get home—the horses lengthened their stride and accelerated their pace.

At dawn, when Jakob entered the family kitchen, Papa had finished breakfast and was reading the *Steinbach Post*. Mama seemed anxious.

"Breakfast?" Jakob nodded.

"Where did you go?" asked Papa.

"*Yantzied*." He paused. Might as well tell him what he wants to know but doesn't want to ask. "Dancing."

Papa folded the paper, rose from his chair and put on his sheepskin coat. "Time to feed the pigs."

[5] "Silent Night, Holy Night"

47

Airplane! Airplane!

THE FIRST VILLAGER to hear the distant hum called the alert, which was then taken up and shouted from house to house. Mama wiped the flour from her hands and joined Papa, who put aside the red hot plowshare he was hammering to step out of the workshop. On each farmyard, men, women and children peered up into the vast prairie sky in search of a moving dot.

"There it is!"

One by one they found the droning speck and followed the aircraft until it disappeared beyond the range of eye and ear.

After the scanty grain had been harvested and the farmer had counted his earnings, an occasional barnstormer might land in a nearby field of stubble to sell airplane rides. The cost of one ride was enough to feed a family for a month. This year, after the worst crop failure in years, there would be no rides. Mostly, the flyers played tag with the clouds and ignored the tiny village where four squares came together on the giant prairie checker board.

But in the early summer a Tiger Moth of the Royal Canadian Air Force made a surprise visit.

It was an overcast and drizzly day when they heard the engine, louder than usual. As the buzz of distant conversation sharpened into words at close range, the hum became a staccato rhythm. The sound circled the farmyard. Now they heard the *pop-pop* of backfire.

"He's looking for a place to land."

The sound faded to the south, then swelled and pulsed.

"He's landing on the summer fallow!"

The yellow biplane dropped out of the clouds and bounced and bumped to a stop a few yards from the village road. When the first villagers reached the craft, two men had climbed out of the open cockpit. One was on the ground examining the landing gear while the other checked the fuel tank.

"Empty. Just made it. We're lucky."

"Everything's okay down here." The man on the ground turned to Papa. "Where are we?"

"The city's about twenty-five miles southeast. Go half a mile east and follow the river south, upstream."

"Can we make a phone call?"

The villagers laughed. The pilot looked doubtful when they said that no one had a telephone but seemed relieved when Papa asked, "You need gas? We've got lots of tractor fuel."

To a villager, any traveler in trouble was a neighbour. The airmen looked puzzled when their offer to pay was rejected.

Grasping the tail of the aircraft, the two men turned it around. One climbed into the cockpit, the other spun the propeller. The engine sputtered and throbbed. The little Moth wobbled to the other end of the field, turned around, paused, roared and took off. It buzzed over the crowd gathered in a circle. The flyers waved and headed east to the river.

1936

Germany sets a world record of 200.4 Km/h (125.25 mph) for a steam locomotive. German troops retake the Rhineland, which the victors of the First World War had given to France as part of war reparations. Italy annexes Ethiopia. Ernest Hemingway volunteers in the Spanish Civil War. King Edward VIII abdicates to marry Mrs. Simpson. At the Berlin Olympics, Jessie Owens, black American gold medalist, is snubbed by Hitler. Returning home, he can't find work and is forced to ride at the back of buses. "I wasn't invited up to shake hands with Hitler, but I wasn't invited to the White House to shake hands with the president, either."

Signor Mussolini and Herr Hitler officially recognize General Francisco Franco as leader of the government of Spain. To establish a joint front against the expansion of communism, a German-Japanese treaty, open to the signatures of other nations, is signed.

Jakob turns 14.

48

Hard Times

ONE SUMMER SUNDAY a young man came to the village and offered his 1924 Model T Ford to anyone who would take it for ten dollars. He drove it back to his village because no one could afford to replace the flat tires or buy gasoline to drive it.

All summer Papa's Model T rested on wooden blocks. The price of wheat didn't matter any more. There was none to sell. The drought and the grasshoppers took all but a few stalks of shrivelled kernels. The bit of grain in the bins would be needed for seed in spring and to feed the horses that pulled the cultivator and the seed drill.

Papa, Mama, Knals, Jakob and the youngest, Petah, sat around the table at *Faspa*, drinking *Prips*. Papa had come home from town.

"Last year we could," he said, as he poured from cup to saucer to cool. Everyone waited for him to say more. "This year we can't." When Papa spoke quietly he was troubled.

"This year—," his voice broke. He bent forward, pulled the red handkerchief out of his hip pocket and blew his nose. "I applied for relief today. I never thought it would come to this. To take charity. To take without giving."

"How much are we getting?" Mama wasn't greedy but curious and anxious.

"More than we need. Much more. Ten dollars and fifteen cents. Every month through the winter!"

Mama gave a little gasp. "What are we going to do with it?"

"I told the lady we didn't need that much but she said it was the smallest amount she could give a family of five."

"What will we buy with it?" asked Knals.

"I bought a bag of flour, sugar and salt. We have our own ham, sausage and bacon. Mama has watered our garden all summer, we have enough carrots, potatoes and a barrel of sauerkraut in the cellar. Next month we'll have money left over. What do you think, should we save some of it?"

"Maybe, for a coat for somebody? Or overshoes?"

Jakob remembered last winter.

"I would like to do that," said Papa, "but it isn't our money. They said it was for food. It wouldn't be right to use it for anything else. And so I bought something special for us and it will still be right. Mama, will you get it?"

She returned from the pantry with a small wooden box of prune plums.

One day, when he was alone with Mama, Jakob asked, "Did you ever see Papa cry?"

She paused for a moment. "Yes."

Like Papa, she would never tell a lie. So he didn't ask why.

"Someday I want to be a weed inspector and drive a new car."

"Jakob, you can't work for the government unless you have an Englaenda name.

49

The Year of Cod

"THE GOVERNMENT OF CANADA has purchased a hundred carloads of Annapolis Valley apples and thirty-five carloads of dried cod to be sent West."

While the Depression was easing in other parts of North America, the Saskatchewan economy took an even deeper dive with the worst drought on record.

Far away across the continent, the men of Newfoundland sailed their boats out on the Atlantic to fish for cod. Those who returned from the sea, and many did not, unloaded and hand-carried the cod in tubs to an area over the water where the head was chopped off, the body split, gutted and washed. After cleaning, the fish was again carried in tubs, above the high tide mark, to be salted as quickly as possible. The salt drew out the water and stopped bacteria from decomposing the fish. The salted fish was, again, carried in tubs up ramps and laid out on racks to dry for up to a month.

Whenever the fishermen were hungry they restored the cod by soaking it in cold water for two or three days, changing the water several times a day.

The dried, salted cod came to Saskatchewan in freight cars, packed in barrels. There were no instructions as to how to get the salt out and the water back in. The hungry farmers pounded, boiled, baked, fried, soaked, steamed, simmered and cooked. The salt stayed in, the water stayed out.

The dogs and cats refused to eat it. Stories were told that one farmer insulated his barn with cod, a hockey player used them as shin pads and another made snowshoes for his daughter to go to school.

Papa shook his head. What if an inspector found the cod in his granary? Would the ten dollars a month relief cheque be stopped? His family would go hungry.

He hitched the team to a wagon, loaded the cod, drove out in the field and buried it.

The coyotes never dug it up.

1938

Enrico Fermi of Italy, wins the Nobel Prize in Physics. Joe Louis defeats Max Schmeling to win the World Heavyweight Championship. Charles Lindbergh test flies the Messerschmidt 109.

Prime Minister Neville Chamberlain of Great Britain, Premier Edouard Daladier of France and Benito Mussolini of Italy meet with German host, Adolf Hitler, in Munich to redraw the map of Europe, allowing Germany to annex the Sudetenland part of Czechoslovakia.

Herschel Grynszpan, a Jewish teenager whose parents are expelled from Germany, assassinates German diplomat Ernst von Rath. In a few hours, thousands of synagogues and Jewish businesses and homes are damaged or destroyed. This night becomes known as Kristallnacht, the night of broken crystal.

Hitler occupies Austria, the beginning of the Anschluss. Prime Minister Chamberlain of Great Britain guarantees Polish borders. Hitler and Stalin sign a pact and divide Poland.

Jakob is 16.

50

The Year of the Turkey

WHEN THE RAINS CAME and crops grew to maturity, the price of wheat dropped from a dollar-sixty to twenty-eight cents a bushel. Eggs were traded at ten cents a dozen for sugar and salt. Doctors were sometimes paid in potatoes or turkeys.

Cousin Aaron Teichrob, whose mother was Papa's sister, was twelve years older than Jakob, married with five children. After some head-scratching, Aaron came to the conclusion that wheat might be more marketable if it was fed to turkeys. He started his flock well before Christmas to take advantage of the *Englaenda* holiday celebrations. His plan went very well until December 26, when the market for turkey prices plummeted even faster and lower than wheat. After three months of turkey roast, soup and stew for breakfast, lunch and dinner, his children lost both appetite and weight.

Desperate, he consulted a *Russlaenda* whom he had found to be of more than average knowledge and experience. Before the Bolshevik revolution, the *Russlaenda* had been a foreman at a brandy brewery in Russia. He quickly discovered that Aaron had all the ingredients for brewing vodka: wheat, a cast iron feed cooker and skill with a soldering iron. With a few feet of copper tubing he had all the materials needed to make vodka. A month or two later, his neighbours noted that strangers from the city visited his farm in shiny new cars, even Cadillacs, Lincolns and Packards.

A month later, Aaron's children had new clothes and came to school with lunch pails containing bread and jam sandwiches instead of turkey. Rumours quickly spread through the community and one day the *Ohms* from the church called on him. After discussing the weather and the crops, they asked if the rumours were true that he was in the business of brewing liquor. They called him to repentance and atonement.

When his wife heard they must stop making vodka she broke down and wept.

"After all these years of suffering and hardship, we have found our way. We have food on the table, our children are dressed, we can afford to go to the doctor and tomorrow I was going to get my teeth done. Now you tell me the church wants to put us back in the poor house. How evil!"

"I know." He took out a handkerchief and blew his nose. "It's not right. But what can I do? You know what happened to Grandpa Schellenberg when he defied the church. The community boycotted him. And it broke up the family."

"But if we can't make vodka, what can we do-o-o-o-o?" she wailed.

And so they prayed all night. And in the morning they dumped all the vodka and washed the bottles. She wept and he cursed. He took the still apart and buried it in the field. By evening everything was clean. They ate, went to bed and prayed and slept.

At seven in the morning they were awakened by a loud knock on the door. In the yard stood a shiny car and at the door were two Mounties in uniform.

"Here's a search warrant. We've come to look around."

And they looked everywhere. In the attic, in the barn, in the granary. They even looked down the hole of the outhouse. All they found was a hundred and twenty-five empty bottles. Sparkling clean.

A few years later Hitler invaded Poland and the price of wheat soared. The war brought prosperity to everyone.

"Our prayers were answered," she said.

Part
five

1939

In February, Japanese troops occupy Hainan Island. In March, German troops move to occupy Czechoslovakia. The Spanish Civil War ends.

In April, Italian troops invade Albania and Germany abrogates the 1935 Anglo-German Naval Agreement. Roosevelt asks Hitler and Mussolini to make a proposal to hold a conference.

From May 17 through June 17, the king and queen visit Canada. Germany and Italy sign a formal alliance. Fourteen German U-boats patrol the North Atlantic Ocean. Germany and the Soviet Union sign a secret protocol dividing Eastern Europe.

September. The German ship Schleswig Holstein shells the Polish naval base at Westerplatte, German troops invade Poland using tanks for quick penetration of enemy territory. England and France issue an ultimatum to Germany and the ocean liner S.S. Athenia is torpedoed by U-boat U30. Over 112 civilians die and World War II begins. Winston Churchill becomes prime minister. Germany invades Poland. Warsaw surrenders. Britain declares war and bombs German warships at Kiel.

The United States issues a statement of neutrality. French troops cross the German border at the "Saar-front." The British carrier Courageous is sunk by the U-29. English children are evacuated from expected target areas. A blackout is imposed and nearly all forms of popular entertainment abruptly halted.

In October, the United States sets up a 300-mile security and neutrality zone around the American coast. The British HMS Royal Oak is sunk by U-boat U47.

November. The U.S. Neutrality Act of 1939 becomes law. Hitler escapes assassination when he leaves a Munich beer hall twenty-seven minutes before an attempt to kill him. In Poland, Jews are ordered to wear a white bracelet with a "Star of David." Russian troops invade Finland.

December. The Finnish Government asks the League of Nations to intervene. The Graf Spee is caught off the River Plate by the British cruisers Achilles, Ajax, and Exeter. The Graf Spee is scuttled off the coast of Montevideo, Uruguay. The captain of the ship commits suicide.

Jakob is 17.

franz, Maria and Klaus

UNKEL FRANZ WAS DEAD. Kidney disease, they said. The orphaned girl he brought home to marry was now a widow. At the age of thirty-two Maria had lost parents and husband and was alone again, now with three sons. The oldest son was eleven, the age when she lost both parents within ten days of each other. Her youngest was four.

Nephew Jakob, now seventeen, was one of six pallbearers at the funeral. Unkel Franz had been a calm man who always spoke thoughtfully and moved deliberately. Except once, when Jakob had been a little boy.

Unkel Franz had bought a new car, Jakob remembered the scent of the new upholstery. Unkel Franz and Papa stepped out of the car, perhaps to look at the field of grain. Jakob opened the door on the passenger side and, propping himself to swing it shut, slammed the door on his thumb. He must have screamed in pain because Unkel Franz spun around and ran to the car to release him. It was the only time Jakob ever saw an expression of alarm or apprehension on the face of Papa's favourite brother.

And now he was dead.

Raised in Rosenheim, where tragedy and suffering was faced with stoicism, Jakob was shaken by the widow's despair. Maria had to be restrained from throwing herself upon the body of the man in the coffin.

"Franz, come back," she cried. "Don't leave me!"

Jakob recalled the words of the pastor, "My God, my God, why hast Thou abandoned me?" *Maybe*, he thought, *God is dead, like Unkel Franz.*

Two years later, Maria received a letter. It was from Klaus to whom she had been betrothed on the boat. He was still single. They married and she had three more sons. One of her six sons took over the family farm. Another went into foreign service. Two became university professors, one a prolific author, historian and sociologist.

She lived graciously to the age of ninety-five.

"I had two wonderful husbands," she said, "and am thankful for my six sons."

At her funeral a story was told of the time she lived alone as a widow. Her neighbours were away overnight, leaving their teenaged sons alone at home. They noisily entertained into the night. Unable to sleep, she made chicken noodle soup and buns.

In the morning she knocked on their door.

"I know you were entertaining guests last night. All that partying must have made you hungry. Here's something to eat."

After Perestroika and the fall of the Berlin wall, one of her sons, a retired university professor, returned to Russia to help the descendants of the revolutionaries who had murdered many members of his mother's family.

52

Minister of de fence

IN SEPTEMBER, Canada declared war on Germany. Western Canada was chosen by the British Commonwealth as one big flying field. The flat and treeless plain under clear prairie skies with two and a half thousand hours of sunshine a year was the perfect place for student pilots in trouble. With temperatures ranging from minus forty to plus forty Celsius, the student pilots were prepared for the heat of the African desert or the cold over the Indian Himalayas to Burma.

One hundred and thirty thousand airmen came from New Zealand, Australia, Scotland, Ireland, England, South Africa, India and Pakistan. Emergency landing fields dotted the landscape. If an engine sputtered to a stop because a student forgot to fuel up or look at the gauge, and if he had enough altitude, a landing strip was always within gliding distance.

Stony Gerbrandt had moved his family to more productive land and he forgot about his stony farm. When the municipality gave him notice to pay his taxes in ninety days or lose the land, he laughed and tossed the letter in the trash. But when the Department of National Defense wanted to buy it for an emergency landing field for the Commonwealth Air Training Plan, he changed his mind, paid the taxes and got a contract to build a high fence around the field.

"So the planes can land without cracking up they're going to clear all the rocks with a bulldozer, to a foot below the surface."

"They won't have to dig deep to find the pilot," quipped a neighbour.

Instead of three strands of barbed wire stapled to willow posts like all the farms, Stony was ordered to fence the airfield with woven wire attached to eight-foot square-cut cedar posts.

"Before, there was no money for anything, now there's money for everything," observed Papa.

After the land was cleared of stones, seeded with grass and fenced, Stony applied for—and got—the contract to inspect and maintain the fence.

And that is how Stony became "Minister of de Fence."

53

Steve

HEARING ABOUT OPPORTUNITIES to earn money after harvest, Jakob rode into town with a villager and caught a north-bound freight train. From conversations with experienced freight train riders, he had learned about the dangers and how to avoid getting killed or losing a leg.

"Try to get on top of the coal tender if you're lucky enough to find one with a decent fireman. But don't let the engine driver see you, he has no choice. If he sees you, off you go. Your second-best choice is to get an empty boxcar. Whatever you do, no matter how cold it gets, don't slam the sliding door. If the latch catches and they dump the empty car on a siding, you'll starve to death. If you have to catch a moving train, try to be on the side of the track where the ladder is at the front of the boxcar. Lotsa guys have been cut in two when they tried to grab a ladder at the back of the boxcar and, as the train accelerated, they swung around the back and lost their grip."

He was lucky to ride on top of a coal tender which gave him shelter from the wind; the watertank below kept his feet warm.

At the last train stop he inquired at a coffee shop and was told he might earn a few dollars cutting timber for utility poles. He boarded one of a string of bobsleds towed by a crawler tractor. Three hours later the driver stopped and gave him directions to the job site, a one hour hike on a snow trail.

After his first shock at the boss' language, he took a liking to Norman. The other two workers acted strangely. When they spoke to one another or to Norman they acted as if Jakob wasn't there and when he tried to make conversation they seemed not to hear him.

On the second day after supper, Norman motioned for him to come outside.

"I'm sorry." The boss looked down and shuffled his feet. Jakob felt sorry for him. "I don't think the fellows want you here. In the bush, with falling trees and swinging axes, well, you might have an accident. Here, I'll pay you for an extra day and you can take off tomorrow."

He held out four one dollar bills.

After breakfast, Norman pointed down a trail that disappeared into bush.

"If you follow that for about an hour you'll get to Steve's cabin. He's an old trapper who's always glad to have a visitor. He'll put you up for the night and you can catch the tractor train tomorrow afternoon."

The two men were watching and listening. Norman's voice was harder than it had been the previous night when they had been alone.

It was a mild morning. The branches of spruce and pine hung heavy with snow. After trudging for an hour, he came upon a small log cabin in a clearing. A man, apparently Steve, paused in his work of lopping branches from a fallen tree and leaned on his axe. His iron gray hair tumbled below his shoulders. Bushy eyebrows shaded his piercing black eyes and a wild beard framed a sunburned nose. His buckskin coat hung over old army pants, the fly half-buttoned.

After a brief appraisal of his visitor, Steve swung the axe into the log and led his guest into the cabin. "I don't get many visitors. I'm building a lean-to for storage. You're soaked. Get your clothes off while I build up the fire."

After his eyes adjusted to the dim interior, Jakob looked around. In the far corner a built-in bunk bed held a bundle of fur. On the wall above the bunk, within easy reach, hung a hunting rifle and a shotgun. A pair of snowshoes. Shelves along most of another wall. Pots, pans, tin cans and salvaged containers held tools, kitchen forks, ammunition and miscellaneous household items.

"Hand me your pants and socks." Steve hung them over a wobbly chair which he dragged to the heater, converted from an oil drum. He grabbed a pail that had once held Roger's corn syrup, filled it with snow and stood it on top of the heater.

"We'll have coffee in a minute. Here, this'll keep you warm." He pulled a black bearskin from the bunk, then seemed to remember something and reached under the bunk to drag out a box from which he picked up an object wrapped in layers of tissue paper. Carefully, he placed it on the bunk and unwrapped a cup and saucer of fine china. He wiped a speck of dust from the saucer and set it on the upended apple box next to Jakob.

"It's from another time and place. It was a different life."

He grasped the wooden handle of his tobacco tin and raised it. Now straight and tall, he seemed to expand and grow. His head up, cup held high, Jakob recalled stories of the Vikings.

"This is now the cup from which I drink." He sketched a slight bow, passing the china to Jakob. "My past. Your future."

He had fought in the Boer War in South Africa and in the trenches of France in the First World War, travelled the globe and now subsisted on a thirty-mile trapline that he checked twice a month on snowshoes. Each spring and fall he rode the tractor train to town to sell his furs and stock up on flour, coffee, sugar, salt, bacon, ammunition and supplies.

"When I get all the shopping done I get a couple of bottles of rum and tie one on. I get drunk enough to last me for another six months."

"Steve, why did those two men hate me? I never did them any harm."

"What were their names?"

"I don't think anyone told me."

"Was one bigger than the other?"

"I'm not sure."

"Blue eyes? Brown eyes?"

Jakob shook his head.

"You didn't see them. There were three and you saw only one. You saw what the other two are. Nothing. Your eyes were mirrors and for that they hate you. It is best for you to keep far away from such men."

"But you see them more clearly than I. Why don't they hate you?"

"I'm alive because I've learned to hide what I know."

That night Jakob slept on the floor between two bearskins. After breakfast, before he set out for the tractor train, he listened while Steve talked.

"I came here to be away from people. I've seen it all, the bad and the good. I've seen men kill men. Done it myself. I no longer wish to hurt anyone or to be hurt. This is the place for me. You're not ready for it. Maybe there's a place for you out there. Try it. Find out. If not, you can always come back. But you have a life to learn."

At the edge of the clearing Jakob turned for a last look. Steve waved and shouted, words that Jakob couldn't hear but understood nevertheless. Steve picked up the axe and swung at the log.

Jakob never saw him again.

An hour down the trail he climbed aboard the tractor train loaded with logs. When the rays of the sun were lost in the shadows of spruce and tamarack, the driver stopped and shut down the diesel.

"If you keep a steady pace you should make it to town by midnight."

The stars were sharp and clean against the midnight-blue. After an hour his legs moved mechanically, rhythmically, detached from the rest of his body, taking him to a place of their choosing. The moon lit up the white landscape, the snow sparkled and the night was soundless except for the crunch of snow under his boots.

He was asleep in motion when the outer fringe of a settlement appeared. The houses were dark. He approached the first, which appeared to be not much larger than Steve's cabin, knocked and was startled by fierce snarling and barking and the sound of a body hurled against the door. A harsh command reduced the din to a low growl.

"Who's there? What do you want?" The voice was not encouraging.

"I just walked in from the tractor train. I've been walking for four hours. Can I have a warm space on the floor 'til daylight?"

"We don't have much room and the dogs wouldn't like it. You can sleep in the barn if you don't smoke."

He approached the largest of three outbuildings and, when he opened the door, inhaled the familiar smell of horse and cow. He made out the narrow windows below the eaves. But there was not enough light to identify his surroundings. Speaking softly to avoid a crippling kick from a startled horse, he grasped a stanchion. Reaching out with his other hand and then, with his foot into emptiness, he groped his way to the end of the partition. The feed trough was wide and long, and deep enough to shelter him from drafts. He climbed in, placed his pack under his head.

He was settling in when a movement touched his leg. He froze, motionless, as it moved up his body to his shoulder, when he heard the vibrating purr. He enfolded the cat and held it close for warmth and comfort. Throughout the night, when the chill awakened him, he moved the cat to another part of his body. Animal and man warmed and comforted each other through the night.

At the first sign of daylight, Jakob gave his companion a stroke of affection and walked to the train station where he had a breakfast of bacon and eggs, leaving him with three dollars.

That evening he slept in his own bed.

1940

Adolf Hitler and Benito Mussolini hold a conference at Brenner Pass; Italy joins the war with Germany. In a lightning action, German troops invade Denmark, Norway, the Netherlands, Belgium and Luxembourg. German bombers set the whole inner city of Rotterdam ablaze, killing 30,000 of its inhabitants. The British Expeditionary Force and the French First Army are cornered at Dunkirk but 338,000 escape across the English Channel. France, Belgium, Holland and Norway surrender. The German troops enter Paris. The six-month Blitzkrieg has cost 27,000 German lives and 160,000 French and British, six for one.

The U.S. limits the export of oil to Japan, which relies on foreign oil supplies. Their stocks dwindle and they look to the Dutch East Indies and Malaysia. U.S. President Franklin D. Roosevelt is reelected for a third term and signs the draft to register 16 million American men.

The first German air attack in the Battle of Britain occurs. The damage is reduced because German bombers are picked up by radar stations, but most of Coventry and Birmingham are destroyed. In less than two months, London is attacked on 57 consecutive nights. Italy invades Egypt and Greece. Germany, Italy and Japan sign the Tripartite Pact in Berlin. German troops invade Romania to "defend" its oil fields. Hungary and Romania declare support for Germany and Italy. British troops defeat the Italian Army in Egypt.

In Mexico City, Leon Trotzky is murdered by an agent of Joseph Stalin.

Although an 1873 order-in-council exempted all Mennonites from state service in time of war, all Canadians 16 years and older must register for national mobilization and each Mennonite must appeal his claim before the National War Services Board.

Jakob is 18.

Adrift

AGAIN, THE RAINS DIDN'T COME. The clouds emptied themselves in the West and drifted, fluffy and white, over the village. The short straw and shriveled kernels of wheat, fit only for cattle feed, were quickly harvested and stacked behind the barn.

Threshing crews would be needed in Alberta where the fields were ripening. Jakob and David, another village youth, hitched a ride to the city. The railway police pretended not to notice as the two youths boarded an empty boxcar heading west.

The rhythm and *clickety-clack* of wheel on rail quickly lulled them to sleep. Daylight turned to sunset, sunset to darkness. Hours later they were awakened by the jolt and clatter of unlocking hitches followed by silence, then the hiss of steam and the *chug-a-chug* of the locomotive fading in the distance.

"We've been dropped off," said Jakob. Three grain elevators towered over a small town emerging in the light of early dawn. "Let's find out where we are. At least we're not out in the country or on some God-forsaken siding."

Except for a dim light in the office, the train station was dark, without a sign of anyone. An empty swivel chair faced an oak desk and a telegraph key waited for the agent. The hands of the clock on the wall pointed at half past four. Around the front of the building Jakob's flashlight picked up a sign over the door.

HANNA.

"We're in Alberta. That must be the highway," Dave pointed to lights moving through the centre of town.

"Should we try to hitch a ride? If we're lucky we can make Calgary before noon."

When the first rays of the sun broke over the horizon, they were in the back of a pickup with Manitoba license plates. The driver and his companion were also looking for harvest work. On both sides of the highway the fields of ripening grain waved and rippled from horizon to horizon, occasionally interrupted by farm buildings. But tractors and combines stood idle in the fields.

The filling station attendant said after two days of heavy rain the fields would need at least two weeks of sun and wind. If not, the best crop in years would rot in the fields.

Late in the afternoon, a friendly farmer, hoping for good weather, offered straw beds in an empty granary and breakfast for a week in return for doing a few chores. Next day the sun peeked out for an hour and retreated behind the clouds.

The farmer took Jakob aside. "It doesn't look good for harvest. Maybe you should head south to Lethbridge and try your hand at topping sugar beets. If you hang around here for another week you'll miss that one, too. You'd best travel by yourself. Motorists don't like to pick up more than one man. If you like I'll drive you to the highway."

In the first hour only two vehicles passed. In late afternoon a two-ton grain truck rumbled to a stop and the driver beckoned Jakob to climb in the cab. Neither tried to talk above the roar of the engine and the rattle of doors until, two hours later, the driver stopped. "I go down that side road to my farm. Better get another ride."

Alone, under open skies from horizon to horizon. Not a building in sight. *Oh well, still a bit of daylight. Chilly, though.* He pulled a sweater out of his bundle, tightened his shoelaces and set out at a brisk pace.

Hardly any traffic now, most heading to Calgary, in the opposite direction. He'd forgotten this was Friday. Family night in town.

Getting dark now. Nobody'd pick him up after sunset. What to do? Ahead, to the right off the highway, a shadowy clump. He crossed the field and circled the straw stack. On the sheltered side, he dropped to his knees and pulled out handfuls of straw and burrowed a cave. Snug and out of the wind, he opened a can of pork and beans and broke off half of a bun he had saved from breakfast. He was curled up and half asleep when he heard a rustle, a pause, a rustle.

Mice. Of course! The stack was last year's harvest. He'd have company tonight. He tucked the remaining half bun in his pack, turned over and snuggled into the straw, ignoring his curious companions.

When he awoke, the cave was brightly illuminated by a strong light from the entrance. The fresh fallen snow was blinding. Although it was already melting there would be no harvest work for at least a week or two. He finished the beans, grasped his bundle and squished back to the highway.

"Where you going?" The driver of the Model A Ford looked about Papa's age, forty-five or so. Well-dressed, probably a salesman.

"Lethbridge."

"Hop in. That's where I live. We'll be there before noon." He stuck out a firm and friendly grip. "Marty's my name."

"I'm Jakob."

"Jake, huh? Hungry?" Noting Jakob's hesitation, Marty laughed. "Today the company will buy breakfast for Mr. Ralph Sandringham, my Calgary wholesaler. Since he's not here to eat it, you'll have to fill in for him. We can't let it go to waste."

"Thank you. I *am* hungry."

How could this man be dishonest? He looked so decent. Yet, he was going to steal and lie. Not for himself ... but to feed someone else who was hungry. It wasn't right, but was it wrong? Could a good person be bad?

"Looks like we'll have to fight the Japs. This guy Hitler's just about had it. Think you'll join up?"

The question startled Jakob.

"They called the last one the Great War. I got my left leg shot off. Infected. It was hell. Nineteen-sixteen, Battle of the Somme. On the first day twenty thousand men died. That year the Somme took more than half a million. Dumb generals shoulda been shot. Instead, they got medals and knighthoods."

The sun was up now, the white landscape blinding as far as they could see. The snow quickly retreated into the shadows of the bushes and then melted as the shadows circled with the sun.

The Ford slowed down and wheeled into the parking area of a motel. "C'mon, let's eat. This place serves great pancakes."

Jakob followed his limping companion into a little café which adjoined the motel office.

"Hi, Marty. What'll it be? Two stacks?" She was a pretty girl.

"Yep. And lotsa maple syrup for my friend here. He's hungry." He reached out and squeezed her rounded backside and she laughed instead of slapping him like she should.

"Ever hear about Social Credit? Premier Bill Aberhart?" Mouth full, Jakob shook his head. Marty had barely touched his plate since they entered the café. "Here, you take my pancakes. I haven't touched 'em." He pushed the plate across the table. Jakob poured syrup over the cakes and dug in his fork.

"Aberhart's a smart one. I voted for him because he made sense. He showed how a dollar in the hands of a poor man circulates. He spends it right away on something and it keeps going. In a month it may be spent seven times or more. But in the hands of the rich it goes into the bank and just sits there and that's why we have a Depression. Money, sitting and rotting."

He lit a cigarette and blew a smoke ring. As it slowed down it grew larger. He blew another, smaller and faster, which drifted through the first. Observing Jakob's response, he smiled. "When you're on the road you have a lot of time to practise."

"After the Social Credit Party was elected, Aberhart set up the Alberta Treasury so he could print money like the other banks. He was goin' to give every man, woman and child twenty-five bucks a month, to get the economy rolling. You know what that bugger Mackenzie King did? He made it illegal, so only the Bank of Canada could print money. He killed the whole deal."

He stubbed his cigarette. "Guess we need another war to get things going. Maybe Hitler will give us jobs, like the Kaiser did in the last war." With his hands he swung his artificial leg over and pushed himself out of the booth. "I see you've finished. Time to go home and see the kids. I've been away for three weeks."

As they entered the centre of town he slowed down.

"Lots of farmers in Lethbridge on Saturdays. I'll drop you off at the employment office. That's where the farmers pick up anyone who's looking for an odd job. You picked a bad day. Not much doing on Satur—" the tires squealed as the car swerved to a stop and the engine stalled. An aging woman, inches from the bumper, unconcerned, hobbled across the street.

"Did you see that? She came right out between two cars! Never looked left or right." The salesman shook his head. "On second thought," he laughed, "isn't she wonderful? She trusts me completely."

After several attempts the flooded engine restarted.

"Good thing I didn't lose my right leg. No reflexes in a piece of wood. She'd be dead."

The employment office was an abandoned warehouse. Weeds sprouted through the cracks of pavement in the parking lot. A dozen men, in groups of two and three, bundles at their feet, looked up expectantly as the car came to a stop.

"Good luck, Jake." They shook hands.

"Thanks so much for the hot cakes and coffee. I was hungry."

The Ford turned the corner and disappeared.

The men returned to their aimless preoccupations, rolling and relighting each other's cigarettes. The youngest appeared to be younger than Jakob, the oldest about Papa's age. Most of the older men looked gaunt, their clothes worn and torn, their faces grimy, hands nicotine-stained and fingernails black. Conscious of his comparative fastidiousness, Jakob turned to open a door marked WASHROOM and collided with a youth.

"Oops, sorry." He might have been a few years older than Jakob. Clean shaven, hair tousled, eyes alive, he smiled easily. "Sam's my name. You lookin' for work, too?" His eyes flicked past Jakob's shoulder. "Let's go! Here's a job comin' up."

A lean middle-aged man stepped out of the stake truck driven by a youth. In another decade he would look like his father who spoke with accustomed authority.

"Twenty-fife cents an hour-r-r. You pick corn. Lots of bending. If you haf a pad pack, don't come." The accent was vaguely familiar but Jakob couldn't place it. The son, who spoke with only a slight trace of accent, selected six men, including Jakob and Sam.

On the half hour ride in the back of the truck, Jakob and Sam lapsed into easy conversation. Sam was a second-year engineering student.

"You should consider an education, Jake. You'd do okay."

"What would I take?"

"Why not agriculture?"

The field of corn, grown to the height of a man, stood in rows an arm's length apart. Each worker was assigned to a row to break off and throw the ears of corn on a hayrack enclosed with wire mesh around the sides and pulled by a tractor. The son towed the rack at a brisk pace and a teenaged daughter followed the workers, checking for any corn left on the stalks.

The farmer nodded in the direction of Sam and Jakob and spoke to his daughter. "*Deh beid, von ehnaunda.*" [6]

Careful not to betray recognition, Jakob recognized the dialect of a Mennonite who had escaped the Russian revolution and migrated to Canada in the '20s.

"No conversating vile you vork." The girl signaled Sam to take a different row, placing another worker between the two friends.

"Slave-driver," muttered Sam as he stepped past Jakob.

To let the men get into a rhythm of motion, the driver at first drove at a moderate speed. Notch by notch, almost unnoticed, the pace quickened. The girl found an unpicked ear of corn and held it aloft. And then another, in a different row. The tractor slowed down slightly, then, rhythm returned, accelerated.

When they stopped for lunch served in the field, the soup was watery, the bread was stale, the bacon greasy and the coffee flat. "A slop-stop," Sam called it.

Jakob overheard the father order the driver, in *Plautdietsch*, to drive faster after lunch. He felt an unfamiliar surge of helpless anger, more for the men who understood nothing than for himself. Through the afternoon the pace never slackened. Each time the farmer yelled or gesticulated, Jakob's anger mounted.

They were resting on the grass beside the farmhouse, waiting to be paid and driven back to town.

Jakob turned to Sam. "Did he say thirty-five cents an hour?"

Sam opened his lips to speak, then formed a half-smile and turned

---

[6] "Those two, separate them."

to the worker beside him, with a light jab of his elbow.

"That's what I heard. You, too?"

With some urging from Jakob, word was passed from worker to worker, accompanied by nods and smiles. The muttering and chuckles stopped when the farmer stepped off the porch with a roll of bills and change.

"At tventy-fife cents an hour-r ... "

In a voice that carried, Sam turned to Jakob "Didn't he say thirty-five?"

"That's what I heard."

"Vot? ... " The farmer turned to another worker. "You heard vot I said. Tventy-fife. Dat's vot I said, didn't I?"

"Nope. Thirty-five."

The farmer scanned the faces around him. Each man returned his glare with a confidence they had not felt for many days.

"I vill tell dem in town. You vill nefer vork around here again."

But he paid. Thirty-five cents an hour.

"If that's how the peasants were abused in Russia I can see why they burned down the barns and houses." Jakob was home and at the *Faspa* table.

Papa saucered his coffee, pursed his lips and with a gentle sigh breathed over the steaming liquid. "That farmer may have lost everything he had. Probably came here with nothing. Borrowed money to buy the land and now counts every penny and nickel."

He sipped. "Life can make a man hard."

"Even a good man," added Mama.

1941

Rudolph Hess, Hitler's deputy and appointed successor, parachutes into the U.K. The details of his mission are sealed, not to be revealed for 75 years.

Within a month, German armies move east into Russia. Japan attacks Pearl Harbor. The United States declares war against Japan and Germany. The Lend-Lease Act is approved. Germany attacks Yugoslavia and Greece. The Yugoslavia army surrenders. German troops occupy Athens. British and Soviet troops invade Iran. Britain and Canada declare war on Finland, Hungary and Romania. Cuba declares war against Japan. El Salvador declares war against Germany and Italy.

55

Schusta Petkau

HE WAS ONE of the five thousand who escaped to Germany from Moscow with the help of President Hindenburg. Three years later, when the Depression had started, he arrived in Canada, a widower with two sons. With the help of his neighbours, he tarpapered an abandoned shack and repaired shoes for the villagers in Reinland. When he asked Mama's youngest sister, a twenty-five year old spinster, to marry him, she quickly accepted.

"Father wasn't happy about a *Russlaenda* in the family," said Mama, "but said she was lucky, at her age, to get any man."

With a strange woman and a crowded workbench in the two-room house, the eldest son took a freight train to Ontario. With employment up, he found a job at Massey Harris, a manufacturer of farm machinery converted to producing military vehicles.

When Papa heard what the youth was earning, he expressed disbelief. "Nobody is worth ninety dollars a month!"

It was a Sunday and the Petkaus, husband and wife, came visiting. At *Faspa* he told Papa his youngest son had joined the Canadian Navy.

"Now he will fight against the Germans who saved us from death in Siberia. And the communists, who killed my parents, burned down our house and took away my sister, only fourteen years old, are supposed to be our friends."

"Have you heard from your sister?" asked Papa.

The guest took a handkerchief out of his pocket and blew his nose.

"Only that she has two children. I don't know anything about their father." His voice broke and tears rolled down his cheeks. "Will my son's ship be sunk by a torpedo fired by those who saved our lives? Will he be drowned by our friends?"

"There is much that troubles me," said Papa. "Canada is now at war against Finland because they defend themselves against the communists. And I am concerned about Jakob. He's the same age as your youngest. He will be called up soon. I don't know what he will decide to do."

"Yes," replied his guest. "I can see he's different."

They both sat silent with their thoughts. Papa spoke.

"What if none of it is true?"

"What we are told?"

Papa looked out of the window. Into the distance.

"Yes. And—maybe ... everything in which we believe."

1942

In this year, the United States produces more than 48,000 planes, 56,000 tanks and, in only eight months, constructs the 1500 mile Alcan highway through the rugged Rocky Mountains. The Japanese invade and occupy islands in the Aleutians, near Alaska.

Canadian families of Japanese descent are shipped to internment camps. Their fishing boats, market gardens and properties are confiscated and snapped up at bargain prices.

Anne Frank gets a diary for her 13th birthday.

The Allies land 5,000 soldiers on the beaches of Dieppe. In nine hours nearly 1,000 Canadians are killed, 2,000 captured and 2,000 returned to England, many wounded.

In Canada, except for Quebec, Canadians vote for conscription, releasing the prime minister from his promise of a volunteer army. An order-in-council provides for young single men to be drafted for military service. Alternative service is available for conscientious objectors in forestry camps where they are paid fifty cents a day plus room and board. Married men with children are exempt.

This year, ten Rosenheim couples marry and, a year later, the village population is increased by ten more children. Obraum already has two children. After nine years of marriage, Knals has seven.

Jakob is 20, the age at which Knals got married.

56

A Wartime City

He'd never seen a mountain or an ocean. Now he was on his way to the West Coast by train. As a passenger. In a day coach.

He had met Jim at the CPR station in Saskatoon, both attracted to a poster. The shipyards in Prince Rupert were hiring men. If they worked at least three months they got free transportation both ways. He'd be trading prairie blizzards for coastal rains and for money to attend the School of Agriculture next winter. When Papa had found out how much he needed for tuition and board and room, he had asked if it wouldn't be wiser to make money instead of spending it? Jakob found a way to do both.

At Drumheller, the steam locomotive picked up a long string of coal cars and in Banff, a second locomotive was added for the haul over the Rocky Mountains. They were now well into the range and, as he looked out the window of the coach, he could see half the train of freight cars and the caboose as they snaked around and over the mountains, over the fragile wooden trestles which connected the tunnels that had been blasted and drilled through the Rockies.

The Alcan highway from Edmonton, Alberta to Fairbanks, Alaska was under construction and Prince Rupert, British Columbia was the nearest Canadian port to Ketchikan, Alaska. American soldiers were everywhere. To make the city a less conspicuous target for Japanese aircraft, the city was under blackout regulation. The headlights of jeeps and trucks were painted over, leaving small slots of clear lens to light up the road directly in front of the vehicle. The tops of streetlights were painted black, illuminating a circle of street around the lamppost. At night, shades were pulled down in windows that had not been painted.

The bombers never came. The only warplane he saw was a P-51 Mustang fighter with United States Air Force markings, which streaked silently past, trailing a blast of sound behind.

Fishing boats were advertised on the company bulletin board for five hundred dollars. A bargain, someone said. Originally bought for thousands, they had been confiscated from owners of Japanese descent who were now prisoners in work camps.

Everything was gray. Rain, rain, rain. The clouds hung low and he never saw the mountain tops which, they said, were covered with snow. Even the gulls were a grimy gray. Herring gulls. Big, ugly and raucous. Not a pure clean white with sharp markings like the Franklin's gull that hovered over a plow in the blue prairie sky. In Prince Rupert, the only bright spots in the landscape were the yellow rubberized pants and coats and hats that kept rain out and body heat in.

When his application showed experience with mechanical machinery, he was assigned to operate a Hyster, a small crane on rubber wheels with a roof that sheltered him from the neverending drizzle.

The employees slept in rows of identical windowless bunkhouses, distinguishable from each other only by a number on the front door. Inside, identical folding tables and benches separated rows of bunks along the outside walls. His bed was the bottom cot of a double decker in bunkhouse twelve.

One day after work, a brawny worker sat down on the bunkhouse bench, rolled up a sleeve, put his arm on the table and looked around the room.

"Anybody wanna arm wrestle?"

With a bit of prodding and laughter, half a dozen men accepted the challenge and lost. When no more moved, he rolled down his sleeve.

"Guess that makes me the champion."

"Could I try?" It was the timid voice of a small man, about fifty, who had been watching.

"Sure, why not?" chuckled the winner. They sat opposite each other and grasped hands. "Say when you're ready."

"I guess I'm as ready as I'll ever be," said the little man.

"I'll go easy on you. What's your name?" smiled the brawny one.

"Joe. Just Joe."

Slowly, the champion pushed Joe's arm until it was an inch from the table. And then it stopped. The big man began to sweat. Now Joe did the impossible. He raised his arm, slowly, until both arms were vertical. Then, without apparent effort, snapped his opponent's knuckles to the table.

"I used to be a circus strong man. You know, bending iron bars. A lot of it was an act that fooled a lotta stronger men. Here's one. It's a trick." He rose from the bench, folded his arms and, legs a-straddle, challenged anyone to pick him up.

He was immovable.

"Okay, what do you weigh?" asked Jakob.

"About a hundred and fifty."

"You weigh less than a sack of wheat. And I can't pick you up! How come?"

Joe laughed. "It's the way I stand. You can't get any leverage."

One evening after work Joe invited Jakob to come downtown.

"On a Saturday night? There's a lot of tough guys out there, drunk. Thanks, I'd rather not."

Joe laughed. "C'mon. It's time you saw some action. Anyway, I promise to keep you out of trouble."

They stepped out of the bunkhouse to walk down the street. The silence of the night was broken by the *rat-a-tat* of the riveters and the flickering lights of welders, reflected from the low-hanging clouds. The shipyards never went to sleep.

The occasional American army jeep or canvas-covered truck with hooded lights rolled by. Other than the narrow rays of light from military headlights, the jet black darkness was broken only by circles of light from half-painted streetlights and the occasional flashlight of a pedestrian. Except in daylight hours, women and children stayed in the safety of their homes.

To keep warm, they walked briskly.

"I think we have company coming our way. Stay on the sidewalk," advised Joe. "Get behind me."

Three men approached. Walking abreast, they took up the width of the sidewalk.

Joe collided with the man in the middle, his shoulder knocking the man off balance. The man on the left swung at Joe, who ducked as the blow grazed his ear.

It was like a circus ballet. One, two and three. The trio was flat on the sidewalk.

"Let's go, Jake. This is no place to hang around." They jogged to the street corner, made a turn and walked briskly.

A mile later. "Okay, Joe, you were a circus strong man. What else?"

"A bit of pro fighting. But I got out before I got hurt."

"That's me, too. If I'd known you were looking for trouble I'd be back in my bunk."

"I never look for trouble. I look for guys who are lookin' for trouble."

"You're on the wheelbarrow today. You'll be pushin' coal in the hold of a new ship. Everybody does it for one day. Just one day. That way nobody gets caught with the job forever."

Which, to Jakob, seemed fair enough.

The ship was being loaded for launching even as riveters were *rat-at-tatting* the reinforcing plates on deck. Cranes swung loads of coal from rail cars, dumping the coal through a hatch into the hold. It was this accumulating pile in the hold that had to be wheeled over planks by wheelbarrow.

For a muscular farm boy this was no problem, but the hammering of rivet guns on the deck above had its effect. For the first time since he worked in the yard he didn't hear the five o'clock steam whistle. The foreman waved for him to quit.

The ringing and buzzing in his ears put him in a belligerent mood for supper.

For a week rumours had been spreading that the caterers were ripping off the workers by selling some of the rationed staples on the wartime black market. Sugar, especially, was in demand by illegal distillers. In the last week the soup *had* seemed to get more watery, the meat tougher, the potatoes soggier and the pie flatter. And the kitchen staff was increasingly rude and contemptuous.

After supper, still hungry, Jakob tasted the pudding dessert, put down his spoon and stood up.

"Anybody want more soup?" Nobody said anything. "Okay, I'll improve it." And he dumped his pudding in the soup bowl, in the centre of the table.

His action released the smouldering fire waiting to explode. They dumped bread, potatoes, puddings and coffee. Anger spread from table to table and exploded out of control. Someone tipped a table, bringing soup, pottery and flatware clattering to the floor. A bench flew out a shattered window.

Jakob hurried back to his bunkhouse from which he observed the flashing lights and sirens converge on the diner.

1943

Isaac Stern, Leonard Bernstein and Duke Ellington debut in Carnegie Hall. Bing Crosby sings Irving Berlin's "White Christmas," Judy Garland sings "Over the Rainbow" on the radio. Poet Charles G.D. Roberts and Sergei Rachmaninoff die. Picasso adds another 23 paintings.

In Moscow, the U.S., China, Russia and the U.K. demand unconditional surrender. The German army at Stalingrad surrenders, the Japanese retreat from Guadalcanal. The Allies land in Italy, A German V-1 missile lands in Sweden. Two hundred and forty-two German U-boat wolfpacks with 10,000 crewmen are sunk. The German army withdraws from North Africa, losing 250,000 prisoners. Italy surrenders.

The bomber which carries Japanese Admiral Yamamoto, who attended Harvard University and planned the Pearl Harbor attack, is shot down by an American P-38 interceptor.

At home, U.S. military personnel go on a 10-day rampage in Los Angeles, attacking scores of Mexican American youth dressed in Zoot Suit style. Detroit race riots take 34 lives, 75% of them black. Desegregation of the 7 million man U.S. Army begins. ENIAC, ancestor of computers with 17 thousand tubes, arrives.

Canadian troops land in Italy and in the next two years have 25,000 casualties and 6,000 killed. Canada offers conscientious objectors noncombatant service in the medical and dental corps. Of close to 9,000 COs, only 122 take advantage of the offer. The others go into forestry camps and other essential services.

The Farmer Student

HE FOUND A PLACE to stay with a widow who owned a two-storey house on University Drive.

As a wartime student at the School of Agriculture at the University of Saskatchewan, Jakob had to attend the Canadian Officer Training Corps (COTC). He took to the regimental marches, the parades and rifle drills easily. There was something about the rhythm, the unison, the sound of the music.

His marksmanship had been sharpened by shooting crows and gophers and rabbits. In bayonet practice, the "enemy" was a bundle of straw hung from the ceiling.

"Right in the gut," yelled the instructor. "And when you stab him in the belly, scream bloody murder. After you stick 'em in the midsection, they're helpless. Leave 'em in the mud, get as many as you can. C'mon, c'mon! Imagine you're stickin' it to a Jap. Picture Hitler as you jab."

When Jakob roared like a bull as he rammed the bayonet into the straw, the instructor smiled because he didn't know that Jakob imagined the instructor as the straw man.

One student who objected to bayoneting said he didn't hate anyone enough to kill. He wasn't seen any more. Expelled, someone said.

Grant MacEwan, the professor of animal husbandry, was a class favourite. "Take a speed listening course before you take a class from him," jibed a student.

Tall and slim, mustached and balding, MacEwan was an impressive figure as he strode into the room, sat down on the desk, swung his legs and launched into his lecture without notes. One hour, nonstop.

"As boys from the farm, you all know about linseed oil, used in varnishes and paints. After the oil is pressed out of flax seed, what's left over is linseed meal, thirty per cent protein, which can turn your cows into milk producers all year round."

Over the Christmas holidays, Papa ordered a sack of meal and within weeks the cows were producing milk. Not as they did on summer pasture, but enough for the family. Papa was silently impressed.

"Maybe," he suggested, "he also has an answer to our disc problem. But how would a professor know more about a machine than those who make it?" He turned to Mama. "If we talk too much about the university people could turn against us."

"Yes, I must not forget what they did to your father."

Professor Ramsey was active in politics and one evening invited several students to his home. Jakob had never thought of milk as an economic or political issue. You got milk by pulling teats. Under the professor's direction, the group did a cost analysis of milk production. They concluded that an average working family of five did not earn enough to pay for the milk that the children needed. Somehow, from somewhere, money must be found and allocated to make up the difference.

He had always enjoyed debating and speaking in grade school and when the chance came to join the debating society he jumped at it. The topic: after the war, would returning veterans decide to farm cooperatively? He won a silver medal and Professor Ramsey invited him to join the Conservative Party after the war was over.

"Not for your political views but for your presence."

The widowed landlady treated Jakob like a son. She didn't seem to need the rental income but it allowed her to continue life in the two-storey home her husband had provided. Although she didn't read, she had preserved the books he had collected and told Jakob to read whatever was of interest. Gradually, he felt a sense of family, of replacing the husband she had lost.

"If you know another nice young student like yourself, he can rent the other bedroom upstairs. You decide whom you want."

And so Hendrick Kasdorf, whom she liked instantly, moved in. On the following Sunday she invited both to join her for a roast. The Sunday dinner became a custom, sometimes chicken, sometimes beef, always with Jakob at the head of the table.

Several times a week the two students took turns listening to her as she reminisced over her family photo albums. It was an exchange for her generosity. When Hendrick expressed impatience to Jakob, he advised, "When it gets tiring, I watch her lips. She doesn't know why I smile. And it keeps her happy."

At the end of the term she gave him one of her husband's books, *Give Yourself Background* by Fraser Bond. It described how a knowledge of classical music, opera, the theatre and great literature can make one at ease in a cultured society, one in which he was beginning to feel at home.

"Something to remember me by," she said.

He never saw her again but always remembered.

Professor MacEwan described the design flaw that caused a one-way disc to pop out of its furrow and how to remedy it. When Jakob returned in spring, before the snow was gone, he extended the hitch and the problem was fixed.

"Papa, we can make much higher returns from our land. And we can start by using one acre of the one hundred acres we turn to fallow every season. We won't lose any production."

"Yes?"

"If I join the Junior Grain Club, I can get registered and certified cereal grain seed. We'd have to isolate an acre so there's no cross pollination with other grains and have it field-inspected several times through the season by the Department of Agriculture. I can get the seed free and, if we do it right, we can get it certified and get very high prices for the grain."

After thinking about it for several days Papa said no. That would give Jakob special privileges which would not be fair to Knals and Obraum.

1944

The Allies land in France, bomb the monastery at Monte Cassino and make the first major daylight bombing raid on Berlin. They enter Rome, Verdun, Dieppe, Artois, Rouen, Abbeville, Antwerp and Brussels. British airborne forces land at Arnhem and lose 7,500 of 10,000 paratroopers. British and Canadian troops capture Caen.

The first UFOs are sighted over the battlefields of Europe. An assassination plot against Hitler by his own generals is foiled. Germans surrender in the Crimea followed by a massive German surrender at Aachen.

Soviet troops advance into Poland, recapture Sevastopol, Minsk and Leningrad after a 900-day siege and begin the offensive against Finland. They enter the first concentration camp at Majdanek, attack Romania and take Bucharest. Finland and the Soviet Union agree to a cease-fire. Soviet troops occupy Estonia and besiege Budapest.

The first German V-1 rockets attack Britain. In Amsterdam, Holland, the Gestapo arrests Anne Frank and her family. Paris is liberated. Allied airborne troops land in Holland. Athens is liberated. Rommel commits suicide. Civil War breaks out in Greece, Athens is placed under martial law. After heavy loss of regular troops, Canada sends its first conscripted troops overseas.

In Saskatchewan, Canada, the provincial Liberals are defeated by the socialist CCF under the leadership of "Tommy" Douglas who has promised hospital and medical care for everyone.

Jakob is 22.

Out of the Village

JAKOB TURNED OFF the engine and the John Deere tractor backfired, spinning the flywheel in reverse. In the sudden silence the ringing in his ears was almost pleasant. The summer fallow was finished.

He ambled to the summer kitchen to wash up for supper.

"Hello, Jeff."

Jeff the Second stretched and wagged a greeting. He'd miss this companion who seemed to understand him. After washing up he skipped up the porch steps and entered the kitchen where Papa and Mama and Petah were seated at the table, waiting for him. They bowed their heads in silent prayer.

Komm Herr Jesu, sei unser Gast,

und segne was du uns bescheret hast. Amen.[7]

"Tomorrow we'll fix the fence. I saw one staple pulled out near the cow pasture." Papa had a sharp eye for things that needed to be done before they got worse.

Jakob drew a deep breath. "I won't be here tomorrow."

"What's more important than fixing the fence?"

"I'm going away. I'm leaving. I won't be here at breakfast."

Papa slurped. "This *borscht* isn't hot."

"I'll warm it up." Mama took the bowl, rose from her chair and refilled it from the pot on the stove.

After salting it, "Much better. It's seven o'clock. Did you wake up Jakob?"

"I yelled at him," said Mama. "With summer fallow finished he probably wants to sleep a little longer. Petah, go and tell him to get up."

[7] Come, Lord Jesus, be our guest and let this food to us be blessed. Amen.

"He's gone," said Petah.

"What do you mean, he's gone?" asked Mama.

"That's what he said last night. I looked this morning. The bed is empty."

"But how did you know?"

"At supper. Last night. He said he was leaving and he wouldn't be here in the morning."

"Did you hear anything like that, Papa?"

"Nothing. I heard nothing."

"I know," said Petah.

Half awake in the gray of the early summer dawn, the crow of the rooster stirred a vague sense of urgency. What was he was going to do today? Something important. The rooster crowed again.

This is the day!

Wide awake, Jakob swung his legs to the floor and reached under the cot. Careful not to scuff the floor, he pulled out the black satchel he had secretly packed the day before with a pair of socks, pants, two shirts and a sweater.

Something about honesty. Truth. This time he would keep his promise. If he faltered today he would never do it.

Silently and quickly, he dressed. Satchel in hand, he crept backwards down the steep stairs.

He stepped on the porch and silently closed the screen door. The rooster crowed. Jeff bounded to him, tail wagging, tongue out, panting with anticipation. The dog would try to follow.

As he walked up the lane to the village street he glanced at the garden, now in full bloom. When would he see Mama's pink hollyhocks against the garden fence again, or pluck a raspberry from the shrubs along the road? Up in a pin cherry tree a robin added his voice to the swelling twitter from the maple grove. The sorrel under the fence was ready to be plucked for *Summaborscht*, with buttermilk and potatoes. No one made it like Mama.

On the street he stopped to look back at the tallest swing in the village. Once, on a dare, he had swung high enough to look over the roof of the house. He had never asked Papa where he got the two telephone poles.

Behind him in the east, a rosy glow spread over the sky. He set off at a rapid pace, conscious of Jeff trailing at a distance. When he reached the end of the caragana hedge which would muffle his voice, he stopped and turned. Jeff halted, ears cocked, waiting to be called.

"Home! Go home!" he shouted with a tone of authority. The dog seemed to sag, retreated a few steps, paused and turned, pleading.

"Home!" He stooped, as if to pick up a stone. The dog fled down the lane.

He looked at his Westclox Pocket Ben. Only four-thirty. He wouldn't meet any villagers this early, this time of year. The seeding was finished and people were glad to sleep, at least until it was time to milk the cows.

Turning west, he swung into a steady rhythmic stride.

He ignored the cows on the other side of the fence, their curiosity stirred by his presence. High in the blue sky, a hawk soared in lazy circles, waiting to make the plummeting dive on a panicking gopher that strayed too far from its burrow.

Three hours and twelve miles later he crossed the highway, set down his satchel and raised his thumb to flag passing cars. Three cars went by, packed with families who would peddle garden produce to housewives in the city.

The fourth slowed down. A '41 Ford, one of the last cars made before the factory turned to tanks and trucks and jeeps. As it swished to a stop on the loose gravel, the window rolled down.

"Where you goin'?" The man in the passenger seat looked about Papa's age, fifty or fifty-five.

"Saskatoon and Regina."

The passenger reached back to unlock the door. "Hop in. We'll get you to Saskatoon."

The driver swung the car toward the highway, gunned the motor to swerve the rear wheels in the gravel, then expertly recovered to point the car down the highway.

"What's your name, young fellah." Jakob caught the driver's eye in the mirror.

"Jack."

"Conscripted?"

"Yep. Going for my medical."

"Not gonna be no goddamn zombie, are you?"

Better shift to safer ground. He wouldn't understand. Papa wouldn't, either. Mama would. She understands most things.

"I had a cousin in the air force. Got killed last year. I don't know where I'll be. Wherever they put me is okay with me."

"George, here." The driver waved his pipe at the passenger. "He was in the navy in the Great War. D'yuh think he should join the navy, George?"

"I'd go for the air force. In the navy it's months at sea on lousy grub. The flyboys get home, get good grub and a place to sleep. And girls, too."

The driver looked in the mirror and snickered. "Young fellah like you'd get whatever you want, eh, Jack?"

His companion laughed at a comment that was lost in the noise of wind and traffic through the windows, now open to the early warming of a summer day.

Approaching the city suburbs they passed the busy airport which Jakob remembered as a flying school with grass landing strips, a windsock and a barn-sized maintenance building, now expanded in all directions with paved runways and hangars. Bright yellow twin-engine Ansons and single-engine Harvards were continuously taking off and landing with a roar. Their pilots would soon be flying Hurricanes and Spitfires and Halifaxes and Lancasters in the skies over Hamburg and Cologne.

Was it a Messerschmidt that brought the flaming Halifax down? Or was it an antiaircraft shell that had obliterated all traces of Archie?

The car slowed as they approached the city centre.

"Your train doesn't take off for two hours. Join George and me for a beer at the King George—we'll celebrate your adventure."

"Thanks." He wanted to be alone, but they wouldn't understand. "Somebody's expecting me at the station."

The car stopped on Twenty-First. "I guess this is it, Jack." The driver reached over the back of the seat. A firm handshake. "Good luck. Your last name?"

Jakob stepped out and looked up the street to the train station.

"Shelly—Jack Shelly."

The End